A NOVEL

TROUBLE'S ON THE MENU

A
NOVEL

TROUBLE'S ON THE MENU

CALEB WARNOCK AND BETSY SCHOW

Sweetwater Books
An Imprint of Cedar Fort, Inc.
Springville, Utah

This is a work of fiction. The characters, names, incidents, places, and dialogue are products of the author's imagination, and are not to be construed as real. The opinions and views expressed herein belong solely to the author and do not necessarily represent the opinions or views of Cedar Fort, Inc. Permission for the use of sources, graphics, and photos is also solely the responsibility of the author.

ISBN 13: 978-1-4621-1093-3

Published by Sweetwater Books, an imprint of Cedar Fort, Inc.,
2373 W. 700 S., Springville, UT 84663
Distributed by Cedar Fort, Inc., www.cedarfort.com

LIBRARY OF CONGRESS CATALOGING-IN-PUBLICATION DATA

Warnock, Caleb (Caleb J.), 1973- author.
Trouble's on the menu : a Tippy Canoe romp, with recipes! / Caleb Warnock and Betsy Schow.
     pages cm
Includes recipes (pages 215–230)
ISBN 978-1-4621-1093-3
1. Women artists--Fiction. 2. Inheritance and succession--Fiction. 3. Community life--Fiction. 4. Organic living--Fiction. 5. Mining corporations--Fiction. 6. Montana--Fiction. I. Schow, Betsy, 1981- author. II. Title.
PS3623.A86434T76 2013
813'.6--dc23
                                        2012050192

Cover design by Rebecca J. Greenwood and Shawnda Craig
Cover design © 2013 by Lyle Mortimer
Edited and typeset by Melissa J. Caldwell

Printed in the United States of America

10 9 8 7 6 5 4 3 2 1

To Tom and Louise Plummer, the BYU professors who
taught me how to write, teach, and live.

—*Caleb*

To Jarom, my better and much more domestic half.

—*Betsy*

ACKNOWLEDGMENTS

I wrote the first draft of this novel a couple of years before I had a publisher. When it came time to offer this novel to my editor, I asked my writing students to comment on the first chapter before I turned in the manuscript. I had a relatively new student at the time, Betsy Schow, who had just finished workshopping a book in my class called *Finished Being Fat* that had been picked up, coincidentally, by my own publisher, Cedar Fort, Inc. Betsy had a lot of really great suggestions for my chapter, particularly for the voice of the main character, Hallie Stone. I found myself writing down Betsy's suggestions as fast as I could, wishing I had thought of them first. The next day, I did what every good teacher does when he is bested by a student—I asked Betsy to coauthor with me and rewrite all of Hallie's point-of-view scenes. Betsy and I then wrote a new ending for the novel, and I'm not too proud to admit that the new ending was Betsy's idea and is much, much better than my original, half-collapsed effort. Betsy, you saved the day, and you did it all on a tight deadline. You are a writer of rare talent and extraordinary voice—and you have become a great friend to me and my family. (We love your weekly yoga classes in our backyard!)

To my friends and longtime colleagues, Cathy Allred, Barbara Christiansen, and Marc Haddock: this book was inspired by you.

Cathy, I hate to say it, but if you hadn't crashed your scooter on that fateful night, I never would have had the idea for this novel!

And to my wonderful wife, Charmayne, who was the original reader of this novel and offered invaluable insight and much encouragement—thank you. Now, if I could only write as well as you do! I love you.

Caleb

First off, I want to thank Caleb for the opportunity to participate in this joint venture. But even more than that, for believing that a writer lived in me at all. Thank goodness people like you don't hog all their talents and hoard them under a bushel. Without your wise and sometimes snarky words, many a writer would be doomed to a purgatory of unfinished manuscripts. Thank you for sharing your time and gifts with me—and for pushing and yelling when I needed it.

A big thank-you to my critique partners from the Wednesday night group—Julie, Stacy, Elaine, Melody, Vickie, Tanya, and Chris. And the CRAP of Utah County—TJ, Karen, and Jessica. You guys have helped me grow in such a short time. You catch things I never would have thought of and cheer my successes.

The biggest thank-you goes to my husband for picking up the slack while I neglected all my wifely and motherly duties to hide in the world of fiction. Thank you for keeping the kids alive while I indulged in my dream. Love you.

Betsy

T*hud.*

Hallie Stone held the brake pedal all the way to the floor well with her foot after the car skidded to a stop. Forcing herself out of the rented Yukon Denali, she fought her way through the biting snow to see what she'd just hit. Her designer heels slid on the slick road. A blast of Montana wind nearly sent her to her knees.

Maybe the blizzard was playing tricks on her eyes. Maybe it wasn't a scooter she had seen, sliding toward the SUV. Maybe it had been only an animal. She'd been warned that moose roamed free up here as numerous as stray cats. But the blur was too small for a moose and too large for a cat. The best she could hope for was a deer.

Please be Bambi. Please be Bambi.

The headlights showed something sprawled on the snow-packed highway. Clutching her puffy jacket—the one practical thing she'd thought to bring from California to Montana—she stared down and saw . . .

A woman.

An expletive popped out of Hallie's mouth—worth at least a dollar to the swear jar back home.

The woman on the ground was making high-pitched keening sounds. An awful grating noise, but at least that meant she wasn't dead, whoever she was. *Thank goodness.*

Bracing in her snow-filled shoes, Hallie stepped toward the woman lying askew on the road. A crushed motor scooter straddled the woman's leg.

"Are you okay?" Hallie blurted. The question was ridiculous.

Fumbling with icy fingers, she tried to find her cell phone in her coat. She had to get help. In the middle of her pushing the nine and the one, a man sprinted out of the darkness onto the road.

Hallie wasn't sure whether to be relieved or to reach for her pepper spray.

"I've called Tug and Jim," he said, kneeling by the injured woman. "Where are you hurt?"

The woman groaned. "My daughter. She's home." She strained to speak. "Mayor, tell her . . . not to worry."

"As soon as I get back to the house, I'll call her," he said. "Don't worry about a thing."

Mayor? Hallie looked at the man who couldn't be more than a few years older than herself. Very young to be mayor.

"I'm so sorry . . ." Hallie wanted to explain how wrong her whole day had been—her missed flight, lost luggage, this behemoth of a rental car that was so different from her sporty Mustang. But the cold was freezing her brain, making her thoughts sluggish and foggy. She wanted to jump back into the Denali and drive home to her Malibu art studio. Or at least back to the airport.

Cutting through the void of the snowstorm, a siren's wail announced the arrival of an ambulance. Slush sprayed in all directions from the approaching tires, soaking Hallie's trousers. Seconds after the ambulance slid to a stop, two paramedics jumped out.

"If I had a nickel for every idiot driver in the world," spat the ambulance driver.

"Oh, Tug," the injured woman moaned weakly. "My leg."

"Probably broken," the ambulance driver said gruffly. "Do I even need to ask what happened?"

"She ran me over!" the woman on the ground cried out with a burst of strength. "I could be dying. I think I see a bright light." She groaned dramatically.

Hallie probably turned a few shades whiter than the fresh powder.

"Naw, just the headlights on the snow," the ambulance driver said matter-of-factly. "Don't worry, Andrea. We'll take care of you."

The paramedics examined the woman and swiftly loaded her into the ambulance. As they drove down the lane, the swirling red lights danced away on the snowy drifts to music of the wailing siren.

Hallie was mesmerized by the light show and lost in her thoughts. On one hand, she was really worried about the women's health; on the other, she was really worried about her own. They didn't throw people in jail for a car accident, right? She *was* an outsider, though, who had just *squished* someone's mother.

I am in so much trouble.

The mayor turned to Hallie. "Maybe you should jump back into your vehicle before you freeze yourself to death."

"She ran into *me*," Hallie blurted, going on the defensive. "It wasn't my fault."

"I know," the mayor said calmly. "I saw what happened."

"No, you don't understand! I was going slowly, trying to find my hotel. I was afraid someone might hit me from behind, I was going so slow." Hallie worked to control the fine quiver in her voice. She was tired, overwhelmed, and pretty sure the wet trousers were starting to freeze to her legs. "And . . . and . . . what kind of idiot drives a scooter in the middle of a snowstorm?" she said, throwing her hands up into the air and losing her footing.

The mayor firmly grasped her arm to keep her from going down. "I'm sure it looked a lot worse than it actually was. Andrea's just shook up, that's all."

She's not the only one, Hallie wanted to say, rubbing the spot on her forearm. It was warm from the man's hand. But she decided not to say anything. She just wanted to find her hotel and get this day over with. She bent to examine the Denali. There was a dent in the bumper. A very little dent. "That's it?" Still, the fist-sized imprint would not make the rental-car company happy.

"This thing's practically indestructible," he said, running a hand along the front of the SUV. "Hitting a scooter with this is like chucking an apple at a concrete wall." He paused and opened the door for her.

Climbing into the vehicle, Hallie cranked the heat up to its highest setting, then reluctantly rolled down her window, allowing the cold to seep back in. "Are the police on their way? Do you think I should go to the station and make a statement?" "There's no one on duty tonight," the mayor said. "We have two deputies out here, thirty hours a week. They mostly deal with warrants and cattle in the road. We're *usually* a quiet place—not much trouble, and not much in the way of a city budget. We can't afford to have deputies twenty-four hours a day."

Hallie gave the man a quick once-over. His smile seemed genuine. Not like the snake-oil grin most politicians wore. Snowflakes began to gather on his eyelashes. He had to be cold. She considered inviting him into her car, but then reminded herself that he was a stranger.

A good-looking stranger—the most dangerous kind.

He offered his hand for her to shake. "My name is Marc Greathouse, and I'm the mayor here in Tippy Canoe. And you . . . you must be here to see our cave."

"Cave?" Hallie had no idea what he was talking about. Nor did she have the brainpower to devote to figuring it out. She was still a little preoccupied with the thought of being charged with vehicular manslaughter. "That lady—you must know her. The woman I, uh, collided with."

"You mean Andrea? She owns the weekly newspaper. *Everyone* knows Andrea—kind of our local celebrity. She's even interviewed the governor a time or two."

Owner of the local paper? Hallie drew a long breath. She'd been in her new "hometown" for less than sixty seconds before she ran over the town's best-loved resident. And the mayor had witnessed the whole catastrophic incident.

Not the low-key introduction to this town she'd planned.

Hallie gave the mayor all her contact numbers as well as her insurance information to pass along the proper channels. Even though he kept assuring her that everything would be all right, she was still worried. But at least she was no longer afraid of being hauled off to jail.

By the time she left and found the Hotel Speleo, snow was coming down in thick, wet flakes, and the wind had died away. She parked and walked into a warm, upscale-rustic lobby with giant timber beams and cozy conversation nooks. A bright blaze in the fireplace cast a flickering light across the room.

Now that some of the shock and adrenaline had faded, Hallie was exhausted . . . and starving. "Do you have a room service menu?" she asked the check-in clerk after receiving her key. "I'd like to have something sent up to my room."

"Sorry," the clerk answered without bothering to look up. "This is the cave's slow season. Room service isn't available past ten o'clock. About the only thing open in town is Plum's Pantry."

The need for sustenance warred with the need to crawl under the covers. As usual, food won out. After a quick change of clothes, Hallie ventured out onto the wintery roads once more.

Several blocks from the hotel, she found the restaurant snuggled in the tiny town's main shopping district.

Inside, there were no other customers. A whiteboard sign at the entrance over Plum's Pantry said, "Now Serving Our Seasonal, Fresh Winter Garden Menu."

Hallie wondered suspiciously what a "seasonal, fresh winter garden" menu could possibly mean in this frozen, snowed-in berg. Snow peas? Iceberg lettuce? She chuckled at her own lackluster attempt at levity. The cold and the late hour were definitely affecting her brain.

A hunched woman wearing an old-fashioned hairnet and green visor slowly wiped tables and straightened condiments. No other employees were in sight. She looked sidelong at Hallie, appearing none-too-pleased to see a late-arriving customer. For several long minutes, she ignored Hallie, making an obvious display of readying the restaurant to close. Probably hoping the newcomer would get the message and go away.

Approaching at last, the waitress asked in a flat voice, "What'll you have?" Her name tag said "Barb."

Hallie smiled, hoping to thaw the woman's cold exterior. "I'd like one egg over-hard and buttered toast, please." The impromptu order was something simple and fast—good for both her and the waitress, who obviously wanted her shift to end. Hallie belatedly realized an egg wasn't going to cut it.

After all the food from the recent holiday, she'd been trying to eat lightly. However, given the kind of day she'd had, surely the Diet Gods would forgive her. "And a slice of the chocolate pie," Hallie added, looking at the whiteboard advertising the specials. "And I'll start with the pie."

Barb brought her the plastic-wrapped dessert on a chilled, white plate and plopped down a fork next to it. Moving to a small grill set against the wall behind the counter, Barb cracked an egg with one hand.

Hallie took a deep breath. The egg cracking reminded her of

the accident. She couldn't stop hearing the awful crunching sound the scooter had made.

Suddenly, she wasn't quite so hungry. She forced herself to take a forkful of the pie anyways. It wasn't bad, actually. Certainly well above standard greasy-spoon fare. Her nerves settled more with each bite.

Chocolate has amazing restorative qualities.

To break the silence and keep her thoughts off the accident, Hallie decided to focus on the business that brought her to this half-horse town.

"So, do you know where I could find Kobold's Trading Company?" she asked the cook. When "Barb" didn't reply, Hallie felt compelled to go on. "I ask because I'm Phineus Kobold's . . .'" She stopped midsentence, unable to say the word *wife*.

Taking a deep breath, Hallie started again. "I'm in town to settle Finn Kobold's estate. I guess he left me his shop—Kobold's Trading Company. Since I'll be here a week or two, I might get to know the menu here pretty well."

She tried to sound cheerful despite the weariness settling into her muscles. After the flight from Los Angeles, the blizzardy drive from Bozeman airport to Tippy Canoe, the accident, and this woman's cold shoulder, Hallie was looking forward to crawling into bed. But for now, she would settle for at least a friendly response.

At the grill, Barb stopped and slowly turned toward Hallie. "You're here about Finn?" Hesitation marked her voice.

Hallie nodded.

"You're a real estate agent?" she said with a pinched look. Clearly that would not be a good thing in the cook's eyes.

"No. I'm here . . . I'm his . . . We were . . . married. Many years ago."

Barb's eyes widened. "A pillar of this town, that's what Finn was. Too bad about his passing."

Hallie wasn't sure how to respond to that. An uncomfortable

emptiness filled the air. Apropos of nothing, she heard herself say, "This is my first trip to Montana."

Turning back to the grill, the woman ignored her again.

"I've never driven in snow." Hallie kept going, unable to leave the silence alone. She had a bad habit of rambling when she felt uneasy. "On my way into town just now, I'm afraid I was involved in a fender bender with one of the locals."

Now she had Barb's full attention. "Who?"

"Andrea, I think was the woman's name. There was someone named Tug driving the ambulance, and he called her Andr—"

"Tug took Andrea in the ambulance? Andrea Linford?"

"She owns the weekly paper?"

The woman gasped. "Is she hurt? *Did you hurt her?*"

"Her leg was, er, broken."

Barb dropped the metal spatula in her hand. "Out," she commanded, removing her apron and spinning the gas grill dial to off. "The restaurant is closed. I've got to find Megan and drive her to the hospital."

Hallie sat motionless in stunned silence, so Barb started shooing her forcefully with the cast-off apron. "Out! You have to leave, now!"

"But—"

The expression on Barb's face left no mistake; any further conversation, as well as the egg and toast, were now out of the question. Hallie debated whether or not to swipe the pie she'd already begun eating. With a tired sigh, she gathered her purse and coat and walked out into the snow.

Great. In the two hours since arriving, she had already dented her rental car, hit the sweetheart of Tippy Canoe, and gotten herself kicked out of the late-night diner.

Let's see what kind of damage I can do tomorrow.

The next morning, Hallie asked the hotel clerk to point her toward the local grocery store so she could pick up some breakfast. Best to avoid the restaurant after last night's unpleasant confrontation. She was still a little unsure whether she was kicked out just so the woman could close or "kicked out" as in banned for life. But that didn't really matter. She had bigger pots to paint. Get in, get out, get home. That was the plan.

In the daylight, Tippy Canoe was even smaller than she first thought. It was much easier to find where she was going without the snowstorm. She tracked down the address on her late husband's estate papers.

Thinking of him that way threw her for a loop. She hadn't thought of him as *her husband* in years, and now she had to add a *late* in front.

Finn had left her almost seven years ago now, and both he and Hallie had moved on and done their own things. After they separated, he came to Montana and made a new life for himself, giving up his art to take over his father's small business. She continued to build her own art career at her studio in Malibu.

Neither one of them had bothered going through all the

hassle and paperwork to make the split official. Hallie was a terrible procrastinator, and because they had no children or joint property . . . well, it was easy to keep putting it off and forgetting about it. Since she hadn't had any desire to remarry, it hadn't mattered.

Well, it mattered now.

Finn had died of a heart attack last month, and it had taken his estate lawyer until after the funeral to track her down and inform her she was still listed as the beneficiary of her estranged husband's will. She wasn't sure how to feel about this unexpected twist of fate.

One thing's for sure, she never expected to find herself in Montana. Cold, blizzardy, afraid-I'll-run-into-a-moose-at-any-moment Montana.

Breaking her reverie, Hallie was alarmed to see the driver of a passing car gesturing to her. *Probably nothing*, she thought, chalking it up to an active imagination. But then another driver did the same, and then another.

Were they angry? Was she breaking some local traffic law? Had someone put out an APB on her rental car after last night's "incident"?

As other drivers passed doing the same thing, Hallie realized they weren't gesturing—at least not in the California sense. The drivers were *greeting* her with a wave or a nod. Using all five fingers instead of just one.

Who knew people really did that? She always assumed those small towns you saw on TV were merely inventions of the state tourism boards, trying to collect more revenue.

When the next driver passed by with a friendly wave, Hallie raised her hand in a self-conscious response. Waving to strangers was unnatural to her and would take some getting used to. Even the people on the sidewalks seemed to nod to her as she passed— which was pretty impressive, considering they should be too busy shivering, walking in the bitter cold.

She had to admit the village was picturesque. Her artist's eye was keen to pick up all the details. Knotted timber planks had been used on many of the stores to create traditional facades, giving the shopping district an upscale and yet Old West charm. Classic shepherd's-crook, cast-iron lampposts lined the streets, and some of the newer-looking stores boasted rustic boardwalks rather than sidewalk.

Then she saw it: Kobold's Trading Company, the name spelled out on a large, neo-rustic, painted sign over the door. Her first chance to glimpse at what she now owned.

And what she was here to get rid of.

Exiting the Yukon Denali, she stepped onto the snowy street, reminding herself to buy the first sensible shoes she found. Heels had clearly not been designed with Montana snow in mind. At least yesterday's blizzard had passed, leaving blue skies, even if the temperatures were still miserable.

Inching across the ice and snow from the SUV to the sidewalk, she made her way to where she could peek through the huge pane-glass windows of the storefront. Baseball caps, souvenir key chains, T-shirts with variations on a cave theme, soda pop and snacks, postcards—the usual hodgepodge that tourists stop to loiter over on their way out of town. Squinting to see deeper into the store, she could just make out a shirt that said "Go Barefoot in Montana," with a large footprint in the middle.

What a crazy shirt. Why on earth would anyone want to go barefoot in the snow?

The shop was locked, just like the attorney said it would be. Shoot. She had kinda been hoping to look around without someone peeking over her shoulder.

Since she lacked any lock-picking skills, she went next door to Cracked Rock, Gems, & Minerals, where she'd been told she could pick up a key. A tiny chime sounded as she entered. Behind the counter stood a slender, younger woman wearing a green turtleneck and ginormous, dangling agate earrings.

"Hello, my name is Hallie Stone, and I'm apparently the new owner of the shop next door. I was told I could get the key from you."

"Honey, the new landlord is here!" hollered the woman behind the counter.

Hallie resisted the urge to cover her ears.

The rock lady turned back to Hallie. "Welcome to town! I'm Melora Post. My husband, David, will be right—"

"I'm sorry," interrupted Hallie. "You must have misheard me. Not the landlord. I just inherited the shop next door, the Trading Post. Or Trading Company. Whatever it's called. Finn Kobold's business."

The woman looked confused. "David!" she called, even louder this time. "Missus Kobold is here about the key to Finn's place!"

"Stone, actually," she corrected. "Hallie Stone." Though when she said it that way, it sounded silly, like Bond . . . James Bond.

"That's right. My mistake. I forgot you and Finn were long-separated," the woman said, nodding. "Finn told us *all* 'bout that."

The smallish woman with the huge rocks in her ears made the story sound sordid—like something you'd see on a morning soap. Hallie wondered exactly what Finn had said. She doubted he would have told *her* version of the story—that he hadn't been able to swallow his pride when her art career took off while his fizzled. That the more she began to make a name for herself in the world of fine art, the more Finn pulled away. For months she watched him become moody and depressed, even more than the normal artist's temperament. He tuned her out, listening only to the demon that whispers in the ear of every struggling artist, the dark voice murmuring that the work is no good and the muse has fled, never to return. In the end, it was Finn that fled.

Absorbed in her own memories, Hallie hadn't realized that a bear of a man had come to the counter and started speaking to her. And there was something about the words he was saying that Hallie did not like. Giving him her full attention now, she focused and repeated the words he'd just said.

The woman who ran over Andrea last night. That's what he'd just called her.

Erg . . . Apparently, news travels directly in proportion to the size of the town. So, given the size of Tippy Canoe, everybody had to know by now.

"I did not run over her," Hallie said, trying for a friendly tone. But it came out a little clipped between clenched teeth. "Her motor scooter skidded into *me*. With the icy roads and all, must be hard to get any kind of traction on those little tires."

"We meant no offense," Melora said quickly. "We just heard about the accident this morning. Poor Andrea. After all she's been through. Hallie, right? Can I get you some coffee? Or hot cider?" She didn't wait for an answer and brought back a steaming cup of something from the back.

The husband moved around the counter to stand next to Hallie and engaged her with a friendly nod. "With the run of bad luck Andrea's had, this is just another kick in the head. It's one thing after another with her." He smiled at Hallie as if prompting a response.

Uh-oh. She could see where this was going. They were settling in to tell her all about Andrea's bad luck. If she didn't stop them now, they might launch into a history of Tippy Canoe that could eat away the whole morning. She had only come to Montana to sell Finn's business—not to familiarize herself with the local drama.

Hallie withheld a long-suffering sigh. She did not want a beverage. Nor did she want to sit around and gab. All she wanted was the key, and she was not above playing up her own drama to avoid hearing about everyone else's.

"I completely understand how that feels. That's why I really want to get into the shop so I can handle all of my late husband's affairs. Find some closure."

Looking into the couple's faces, it was clear to Hallie that they were disappointed in her unwillingness to mull over the details. She felt guilty about playing the dead husband card, but she was determined to deal with the estate as quickly as possible and then go back to her brushes and her paints in Malibu. She was determined to put Finn behind her. The contradiction of trying to do in one week what she hadn't managed to do in seven years was not lost on Hallie.

Melora finally gave a sympathetic nod and retrieved a single key, which was attached by a leather tog to a piece of antler at least as long as Hallie's forearm. The words *Kobold's Trading Company* had been artfully painted in what Hallie recognized, after all these years, as Finn's chunky handwriting. An unexpected sadness welled up in her.

Where had that come from? It was time to do what she'd always done: box up the feelings and store them to release into her art later. Thinking about this now would do no good. And besides, big girls don't cry—especially in front of strangers. She coughed away the emotions that were choking her and stood up to leave.

"I'll run next door with you and introduce you to your tenants in the other two stores," Melora said.

Did this woman have rocks *in* her ears as well as hanging off them?

"I don't think you understand," Hallie said, speaking slowly out of sheer exasperation. "I'm not the new landlord. I only own what Finn owned. The store next door."

"Finn owned Christiansen's," Melora gently corrected, also speaking slowly as if Hallie was too dense to understand what was being said. "That's the building we're standing in. Way back, this building used to be Christiansen's Department Store, where everyone came to order in their clothes and appliances from the Sears Roebuck catalog."

"Back in the day, Finn's father subdivided the place into four smaller storefronts," David added. "Everyone in town still calls it Christiansen's. Except the tourists. They don't know any better."

A dim lightbulb in the back of Hallie's mind started to brighten. The name *Christiansen's* sounded awfully familiar. It might have been mentioned by the attorney who had spoken to her over the phone. Between shock and bad cell phone reception, the conversation had been spotty. A sinking feeling in the pit of her stomach said she was about to learn that her responsibility here was much larger than she'd understood.

"Finn kept one store for himself and rented out the other three," Melora said. "Besides our rock and mineral shop, there's Tumpi's Pizzeria two doors down and the Frost Shoppe next door. Just so you know, ours is the smallest of the four."

Hallie wasn't sure why it had been important to mention the size of the rock shop, but she had a sneaking suspicion that the logic linked somehow to the rent payment.

"The key you're holding was Finn's master key for all four storefronts," David said.

"So you see, you *are* the new landlord. Or landlady, if you'd prefer," Melora said cheerily.

Not for the first time since arriving in town, Hallie found herself needing to sit down to stop the room from spinning.

Outside Cracked Rock, Hallie read the sign over the store next door. "The Frost Shoppe—Home to the World-Famous Huckleberry Thickshake." She followed Melora inside, where there were at least a dozen customers. The menu boasted a small lunch selection and shakes in many flavors Hallie had never heard of—buffaloberry, tayberry, gooseberry, anise, raspberry fudge, pumpkin eggnog, fresh watermelon. There was even a specialty flavor called, "Buffalo Chip Supreme."

Hallie shuddered. That was just wrong.

Melora greeted two teens at the counter with a wave and a question. "Judy in the back?"

One of the teens gestured toward the rear of the store, and Hallie reluctantly followed Melora through a fingerprint-marked, stainless steel door tucked between a wall and a large freezer. Inside was a small room. A very plump woman with a wispy bee-hive of hair piled on her head sat at a desk, tapping on a business calculator with fingernails that were at least two inches long. Painted with flowers. With rhinestone centers.

"Melora, darlin'," the woman said enthusiastically. She rose up, engulfing the much smaller woman in a hug. "Who's this you've brought in with you today?"

Melora introduced Hallie as the new owner, and Hallie found herself unwillingly gathered into a bear hug as well.

There was no time for Hallie to feel awkward about the contact; she was too busy struggling for air while being smothered by the lady's polyester-covered bosom.

"Hallie, this is Judy Frisk," Melora said. "Judy also owns Honeysuckle Salon, about a block from here."

"Darlin', a Big Sky Montana welcome to you," Judy chirped, finally letting go and batting thickly mascaraed eyelashes. Her eyes were so intensely blue that Hallie suspected she wore colored contact lenses. Or that she was an alien. Given Judy's odd fashion sense, neither answer would surprise Hallie. "I'm so happy to finally make your acquaintance. So sorry about Finn. He was a dear. Just a dear. We all loved him so."

Hallie decided not to read anything into that last part. Little late to start feeling jealous now.

"First thing's first: you've got to taste the wares," Judy said, her beehive bobbing up and down. "Come on out front with me, and I'll whip you up a thickshake like you've never seen. You're gonna just love it. Love it! Have you ever tasted buffaloberry before?" She didn't even pause for an answer. "You have to try this. A Montana delicacy!" Judy began scooping small red berries into a large stainless steel cup.

"Sure, I'll try it," Hallie said. Not that she really had a choice, it seemed. "But please, just a small sample for me. I'm sure I'll love it." *And if not, I'll try really hard not to spit it out*, she thought. For some reason, the name buffaloberry brought unwelcome images of buffalo anatomy to mind.

Judy was scooping hard vanilla ice cream now. That was encouraging. Can't go wrong with vanilla.

"The Frost Shoppe is famous for making up shakes that are thick enough to stand a spoon in," Melora said, speaking loud enough to be heard over the sound of whirring blenders. "And for memorable flavors."

Hallie hoped "memorable" wasn't a euphemism.

When Judy finished the shake, the pale ice cream had been transformed into a crimson color. Not the most appetizing shade in the world, unless you're a vampire. Hallie fought to keep her face straight as she ventured a bite.

Thank goodness it tasted better than it looked.

"It's good," Hallie mumbled with her mouth full, honestly surprised. "It's different. Tangy. I like it."

Judy looked both pleased and relieved, which was a little odd. Did she really care that much if Hallie liked her shake?

When they left the Frost Shoppe, Judy made Hallie promise to visit Honeysuckle Salon for "a hairdo on the house." Hopefully not everyone who visited the Honeysuckle Salon came out with a beehive.

"I don't know how Judy manages two stores and two unruly teenage boys by herself without going insane," Melora whispered conspiratorially as soon as they were out of earshot.

The hairdo and crazy fashion sense indicated that insanity may indeed have crept in, but Hallie didn't say a word.

Melora took that as permission to launch into yet another chapter of the Tippy Canoe drama. "But I think she's really better off without Kenny. Good-for-nothing waste of oxygen, that man. Drinking, gambling, women . . . the whole nine. No surprise she got everything in the divorce. The kids, the stores, the house . . . the dog! The only thing she gave back to him was his stupid last name. Who'd want to be named Petrolo anyway. Sounds like the name of an oil comp—"

"Oh look, we're here." Hallie pointed to the sign saying Tumpi's Pizzeria—effectively putting an end to this episode of *As the Canoe Tips Over*. Painted lettering on the windows announced, "Homemade root beer served in ice-cold mugs," and, "Made-to-order sourdough calzones and pizza, made with natural yeast. The old way."

A warm swoosh of pizza-and-mozzarella-scented air hit Hallie when she stepped through the door. Melora introduced her to Peter Tumpi and his wife, Isabelle, who were taking orders at the counter. Both husband and wife greeted Hallie with a kiss on each cheek, something she hadn't expected in Montana. She couldn't quite place their accent and wondered aloud if it was an Italian dialect.

"Slovenian," Isabelle said.

Hallie's blank stare must have given her away, because Isabelle followed by saying, "We come of Slovenia. Very small country on Italy North. I'm no surprise you don't hear of it. Many Americans not ever hearin*ck* of it, I think."

"But our pizza aims to be the Italian," Peter said, his accent much easier on the ears. He was a short man, actually shorter than his wife by about two inches. He had broad shoulders, thick arms, and a barrel chest.

For her part, Isabelle was a thin slip of a woman, wearing a folded handkerchief to keep her hair out of her eyes. "Please, sit down and I'll brin*cking* you both a pizza slice. *Quattro formaggio*— four-cheese pizza. How that does sound?"

When Hallie didn't answer right away, Melora answered for her. "Actually, we saw a slice of tomato pizza on someone's table when we came in. Would it be too much trouble to try that instead?"

So Melora had noticed Hallie glancing longingly at the plate. It had looked amazing, and it had taken real effort not to sneak a bite as she passed.

"*Quattro formaggio con* sliced tomatoes. For you both?" As Melora nodded yes, Peter moved toward the kitchen, speaking the order to someone Hallie could not see.

The pizza tasted wonderful—a savory, guilty pleasure. Hallie was hungry, despite starting with dessert at the Frost Shoppe. When Isabelle offered her a second slice, Hallie did not protest. She could always count the calories in place of the dinner she'd missed yesterday.

"You lova, yes?" Isabelle said, hovering. "You no raise the rent, then, yes! Pizza good, rent good!"

I don't even know what the rent is, thought Hallie. *I don't want to know.*

Why was it that all of her tenants—she still couldn't get used to saying that—seemed to be preoccupied with the rent? Was that why they were all giving her good food—to soften her up? It wasn't going to be her problem, but if it was, the tactic might actually work. *Yum*, she thought and swallowed the last bite.

After finishing their food, Melora insisted that they cross the street to meet the neighbors even though they had now officially met all of the tenants. When Hallie implied that her head might explode if she had to learn one more name today and that tomorrow would be better, Melora said, "Better to just get it all done at once. My dad always said 'Best to start with a firm handshake and a solid look in the eye.' Wouldn't you agree?"

There was really no way to disagree without seeming like a total jerk, so Hallie decided to continue to follow Melora's lead.

Their first stop on the extended tour was the adjoining shops named, "His: Tackle & Outdoor" and "Hers: Chocolates & Confections." Inside, Hallie found there was an arched pass-through between the common wall, allowing browsing customers to move seamlessly between "His" and "Hers."

Clever. And cute. And not in the overly done, "I want to throw up" kinda way. The distinct aroma of chocolate filled the air in both stores. Chocolate always made a good first impression.

"The stores are owned by the sweetest married couple, Mathew and Brooklyn Teasdale," Melora said. "Brooklyn and I actually grew up together in Tippy Canoe. We went to the Tippy Canoe Academy together, grades K through 12 all in one building. She met Mathew—" She broke off, as a very pregnant woman approached. "Brooklyn, you are the picture of motherhood!" She introduced Hallie. "Now, Brook, you're due when? In three weeks?"

"Just about," Brooklyn said, rubbing a hand on her belly. "It won't be a minute too soon. I'm ready to get this girl here." She grabbed her stomach gently with both hands, chuckling. "And outta *here*."

Brooklyn showed them around the chocolate shop, pausing to let them watch as a woman named Julie deftly manipulated glistening, molten chocolate on a stainless steel table. In rapid movements, she kneaded and folded the chocolate. The work was fascinating to watch. It was a stroke of real genius to allow the customers to watch the chocolates being made by hand. *I know it's whet my appetite*, thought Hallie.

"Julie is an expert at getting it to just the right consistency," Brooklyn explained. "When it's just where she wants it, she'll separate it into smaller batches on the warming table and add specialty flavors. We sell green tea, peach nectar, cinnamon, white pepper—all kinds of fun, unusual flavors. And we have the more traditional stuff too for the people who crave that."

Of course you can't have an introduction like that without having a little taste test. And who in their right mind would pass up free chocolate samples? Even after a shake and two slices of pizza.

Hallie started with a peach nectar confection, which was too syrupy and sweet for her taste, though she didn't say so. The white pepper–chocolate combination was shockingly good.

"Honestly, it's not a flavor I could have ever dreamed up, but the spice and the chocolate work really well together." Add a point in the column for trying new things.

She purchased a half-pound of English toffee, always her far-and-away favorite. Wasn't it everybody's? The version sold in this shop was buttery and smooth, and not too rich. An excellent toffee.

Hallie was given only a brief introduction to Mathew, who was deep in discussion with two men, giving them advice on "flies" for fly-fishing and showing them options. Each tiny ersatz insect was different—some brightly colored, some done in more natural hues. Some had long, jutting tails, while others consisted only of little puffs of fur or feather.

"The section over on the left are the ones he's made by hand," Brooklyn said proudly as they made their way toward the front doors.

"He gives demonstrations every Tuesday and Thursday," Melora said. "I actually tried it once. The flies are fun to make. But since I don't fish, I couldn't find much use for them except maybe as earrings!" All three women laughed.

Hallie's mood was high after sampling all those delicious chocolates, but it sank the moment she recognized where they were going next.

If I curse in my mind, Hallie wondered, *do I still owe a dollar to the swear jar?*

Last night, Hallie had been too tired to notice much about the diner she'd been kicked out of. Now that she was awake, she could see it was much nicer and larger than she remembered it. Plum's Pantry was a sprawling, family-style restaurant, decorated with Montana-themed heirlooms—copies of historic photographs in barn-wood frames, antique skis, withered-looking snowshoes with gnarled leather straps, and old Montana license plates.

And moose. Lots of moose stuff.

Yeck! What was it with Montana and moose?

When Hallie was a child, there'd been a traumatic incident with a moose. Ever since then, they freaked her out. Wasn't much of a problem in California. But here, everywhere she looked . . . *sigh*.

"We wanted to say a quick hello to Bob and Betty," Melora said to the woman who greeted them at the door. Her name was "Staci," and thankfully Barb was nowhere in sight.

Hallie decided to keep her mouth shut about getting kicked out the night before.

"Plum's is a long-time local icon," Melora said. "Famous far and wide because almost everything they serve is grown year-round and organically right here in Tippy Canoe. They have these huge, geothermal greenhouses where they grow stuff all winter for the restaurant. They give tours and everything. Big, fancy magazines have been here to do stories, even."

So that is what "seasonal, fresh winter garden menu" had meant, thought Hallie. She'd never heard of a geothermal greenhouse. She wanted to ask if that meant a greenhouse heated by a volcano but decided to hold her tongue.

She followed the hostess, expecting to be shown into a back office or even the kitchen. Instead they were taken to a worn corner booth.

Oh please. Not more food, Hallie panicked to herself. If she ate anything else, she was likely to pop. Or at the very least be forced to unbutton the top of her pants.

"We're not actually eating," Hallie said quickly. "I just wanted to meet the owners. I'm the new owner of . . ." She looked at Melora for confirmation. "Christiansen's, across the street."

A minute later, an elderly couple joined them. Hallie guessed they must have been in their seventies. He used a wooden cane, carved with images of wildlife. The artistic side of her appreciated the craft and intricate carvings, but the nature-phobic side of her did not care for the moose and elk design.

"Bob and Betty Greathouse," Melora said as they took a seat. "Meet Hallie Stone, the new proprietor of Christiansen's."

Bob Greathouse—the name was familiar to Hallie. But she just couldn't pin it down.

"Glad to meet you in person," Mr. Greathouse said. "After our chats on the phone."

"You're the attorney," Hallie said.

The very attorney who had tried over the phone—in wandering sentences full of "When I was a boy" references—to explain what Finn left her to take care of. *Obviously the extent of the message hadn't quite come through,* Hallie noted wryly.

"Yep, not just a restaurateur, he is also Tippy Canoe's only attorney-at-law," Melora said.

"We're also owners of the two gas stations in town," Betty said with pride. The couple beamed.

Hallie noticed that the pair was holding hands when they approached the table. They were still tightly clasped, and, occasionally, one age-spotted hand gave the other wrinkly hand a shaky squeeze. The pose looked so natural that it was clearly a long-established habit. She wondered if they even realized they were doing it or how sweet they looked together. This would be nice to have—someone to hold hands with in life. Someone who would walk by her side, holding her hand out of loving habit. If she let her mind wander just a smidge, she could almost picture it.

Bob was gesturing for a server. "Bring us a couple menus, please."

"No, that's all right," Hallie said, pulling out of her daydream. "We've already been fed every place we've been."

"We'll share a Scottish egg salad with a popover and peach-cantaloupe preserves," Melora overruled.

Hallie stared at her companion in disbelief. This woman had eaten just as much as she had. And she was so darn skinny too. Where on earth did she put it all?

Melora just grinned back. "Trust me."

Well, Hallie didn't want to be rude, and maybe just a bite or two wouldn't hurt.

The salad that arrived at the table was made up of the usual ingredients, topped with a hard-boiled egg that had been wrapped with a thin layer of sweet Italian sausage, baked, and then sliced. On a separate plate came a steaming popover smothered in butter and golden-orange preserves.

Happiness on a plate. That's what they should have named this dish. Hallie could see why Plum's had been a mainstay in this town for generations.

As they ate, Bob—he insisted Hallie call him that—confirmed that Hallie was indeed the new landlady to all four storefronts that had once made up Christiansen's Department Store.

Hallie was startled to feel a warm hand on her shoulder.

"Well, hello, Marc," Bob said.

"Hello, Grandpa Bob."

The voice sounded familiar, and now Hallie remembered where she had heard the name Greathouse recently. She titled her head all the way back and looked up. Standing behind her chair was the man who'd helped her the night before. And she was giving him a perfect view of the insides of her nostrils. Wonderful.

Marc smiled down at her. "Quite an evening you had yesterday. How are you feeling today?"

In the daylight, Hallie could see that the mayor was not mayorish-looking at all. In fact, he was quite attractive, with a defined jaw line and great hair, worn slightly long. Handsome and rugged . . . if you go for that sort of thing.

"I'm fine, thank you," she answered. "How is that woman? Andrea, I think her name was."

"She's already resting at home. Doctors said it was a clean break, which makes it easier," Marc said. "And Andrea's a fighter." He turned, chuckling. "Pop, you should have seen this last night. Andrea was out riding some tiny little motor scooter she bought in Bozeman, hit a patch of ice, and slid right under this woman's SUV."

Hallie was relieved to hear someone else tell the story the way it actually happened.

"And don't you know," the mayor continued, "there's Andrea, lying on the ground with Tug and Jim working on her, and first she's worried about who'll tell her daughter, Megan, what happened. Weak, barely able to lift her eyes. Then, in the next breath she's hollerin' and flailing, accusing this woman of trying to kill her, and moaning about passing on." Marc looked at Hallie. "I hope you don't mind me saying so, but the look on your face when

Andrea said that to you—well, it was one of the funniest things I've seen in a long while."

"I suppose I'm glad somebody got a laugh out of it," Hallie said. "But truly, I'm grateful you were there to witness what happened. And help sort out the mess."

"My dad's a deputy here in town—one of only two deputies in Tippy Canoe. I was headed over to check in on him anyway, and I told him everything I saw and filled out a witness statement. Dad said not to worry too much. Andrea's not the type to file a complaint."

"Thank you," Hallie said. "You don't know how much better that makes me feel."

Good-bye, visions of orange prison jumpsuits.

"It seems like the Greathouse family is something of an institution around here." Hallie found herself wanting to extend the conversation with this man. Unusual, since so far she had been stoutly trying to avoid any unnecessary backstory of this town.

"That it is. Been around here since the founding. There might be a Greathouse in the mayor's office, but it's Grandma and Grandpa Greathouse here that keep the town running with their good food. I think Tippy Canoe would riot if they didn't get their weekly fix of popovers." Marc chuckled and looked fondly over at Bob and Betty, who blushed.

Marc again homed in his attention on Hallie. "I don't believe I ever got your name last night."

"Hallie Stone. Visiting from Malibu, California. I'm . . ." She shot Bob a pleading look for help.

"She's inherited Christiansen's," Bob said matter-of-factly. "She's Finn's wife, though they'd been estranged for a number of years, if I understand correctly. She's in town working with me to dispose of the estate."

Marc nodded solemnly. "Finn was salt of the earth. A great guy who will be missed."

There was nothing Hallie could think of to say to that. Her

feelings about Finn were too conflicted to explain to herself, let alone share with strangers.

"I'll let you two get back to your legal business," Marc said as his pocket started buzzing. And then to Hallie, "Every storefront in town is important to our little downtown economy. Let me know if there's anything you need." He grabbed a napkin and scribbled down his number, leaving it next to her. "I'm always around. Pop knows how to find me." And with a parting nod to Bob, Marc left to answer his phone.

Even though Hallie was sorely out of practice, she thought she detected a hint of flirting. Seemed like a good man. And funny. Not to mention easy on the eyes.

While Hallie had been focused on Marc, Merlora had been busy planning out the rest of Hallie's day.

"After we finish here, I was thinking we could stop by Made-In-Montana," Melora chatted animatedly. "It's a little shop on the block north of us, owned by a great woman named—"

Hallie cut her off. "Thank you for everything, but I really don't think I could possibly remember any more names or faces today. Not to mention I'm about to go into a food coma." She hoped her tone showed good humor, not irritation.

It was a good thing she'd branched out and met the neighbors even though she hadn't wanted to. She'd had a good time, even more than she was willing to openly admit. But more important, any one of the local business mavens she'd met today could very well be the one who decided to take Christiansen's off her hands. Yes, she had really liked the quaint little town so far, but she was still determined to get back to her own life. She focused again on the task at hand, ignoring the tasty and handsome distractions of the day.

"Bob, now that we're about finished with this *delicious* food—and I mean that sincerely, it really is delicious—"

Bob and Betty beamed.

"—I'm thinking I ought to meet with each of the tenants this afternoon." Hallie paused. "I'm not in town for long, so I'd like to get a better handle on all this landlord business. Rents, leases, contract, and such. I could use some help. Would you be available to sit in? We could start at Cracked Rock with Melora and David, if that's okay with everyone."

"I don't see that being any problem at all," Bob said, looking at his wife, who did not disagree. "And I think you're right. Everyone's bound to have some questions about the future."

"It would be good to have a chance to talk business, now that you've met everyone," Melora said. "I'd be lying if I told you we haven't wondered if you'd be wanting to make changes. We had a special deal with Finn when it came to rent." Melora turned to Bob. "Have you told her about our rent situation?"

Special deal? That couldn't be good.

"The alfalfa hay?" Bob said. "No, I didn't have a chance to tell her that."

That *really* couldn't be good.

Hallie got the full explanation later at her meeting with Bob, Melora, and David at the Cracked Rock.

"Finn had a few mares and a stallion he got from his dad," David said. "We've got a small farm, and we had an agreement with Finn where he'd let us pay quite a bit of the rent in hay."

Hallie shot a panicked look at Bob. Did she inherit horses too? She was pretty sure there was no mention of horses in their phone conversations. And all the ghosts of goldfish past could testify that Hallie was not good with animals.

Bob must have correctly understood the look, because he said, "Finn had an understanding about the horses with a neighbor. They aren't part of the estate."

Phew. At least that was one less thing to worry about. But it looked like there was still plenty.

Melora and David were looking at the floor. Not a good sign.

She certainly couldn't be expected to continue letting them pay rent with hay. Especially since she—thankfully—didn't have any horses.

"Business around here is in the dumps with the economy and silver mine shutting down," David said bluntly. He gestured toward the front of the shop. "As you can see, not many people are pounding down the door."

"I think what David's getting at is that rent for Cracked Rock, The Frost Shoppe, and Tumpi's is halved during the months of December, January, February, and March," Bob said solemnly.

"Owing to the fact that these are, by far, the slowest months of the year," David said earnestly.

Melora stopped fiddling with her coffee cup and looked up as well. "Most of us only open our stores for reduced hours, if at all. The slow winter is kind of like our vacation. If we want to close our store to go out of town for a week, winter is the time to do it."

Hallie could see they were trying to break the bad news to her gently. "Let me be straight forward, if I may," she said. "I'm a working artist based in California. I'm not really looking to be a business owner in Montana. I'm in town to find a buyer for . . ." She flew her hands around trying to encompass all of her new-found holdings. "Let's not worry about this for now, and you discuss the rent situation with whoever the new owner will be."

If she could find an owner. She had a nagging feeling that finding someone to buy an ancient building in a tiny, quiet town where the rent was paid in alfalfa hay might not be easy.

Or fast.

"Darlin', it's like tryin' to shoot spit from a pistol 'cause you've run out of bullets," Judy Frisk said in her loud voice, gesticulating dramatically with her hands as she spoke. "I mean, business just dries up over the winter. This place"—she gestured to the Frost Shoppe, where Hallie and Bob were seated now—"does a fifth the business over winter compared to what we take in over the summer."

"But you're not paying rent in hay?" Hallie meant the question for Judy as a jest, but she looked at Bob.

"Thickshakes are mostly what Finn had a hankerin' for," Judy said. "Especially in summer. Not a day'd go by that Finn wasn't in here gettin' me to whip him up a Buffalo Chip Supreme. And most days he'd have a burger and fries too from our lunch grill. And did I blame him for not wanting to cook or eat alone? No. He was a bachelor . . ."

Hallie could see it had begun to dawn on the woman what she was saying. Finn had not been a bachelor—not exactly. *Maybe if we'd just gotten a divorce, I wouldn't have to be here right now in this frozen, forsaken place*, Hallie thought. *I'd be home in Malibu , enjoying the beach or painting from the natural light in my studio overlooking the steel-gray ocean as it reflected the clouds.*

And I'd be warm.

"Finn kept a running account at both the Frost Shoppe and Tumpi's," Bob said. "At the end of the month, his bill was deducted from the rent."

The mystery of how a relatively healthy middle-aged man died of a heart attack was starting to clear up. Especially if he accepted most of his rent payments in artery-clogging food.

Hallie wondered aloud whether the unusual rent agreement might make it more difficult to find a buyer for the place.

"Is that what's eatin' at you?" Judy waved away Hallie's concern. "Don't's you worry none. T'wouldn't be any harder. Not with times being what they are right now in Tippy Canoe. It'd be tough no matter what."

Hallie wasn't sure that she liked the way Judy had phrased it. Or that what Judy was implying was good news.

Hallie had planned to visit Tumpi's next, while she had Bob at her side to help her manage technical questions. But now she changed her mind. She could feel a migraine coming on.

She couldn't bear to hear any more about rent paid in thickshakes and hay.

Taking emergency ownership of Dad's Christmas tree farm was not on my priority list of things to do this winter, thought Marc Greathouse.

As mayor of Tippy Canoe, he had a full plate dealing with the aftermath of the defunct silver mine—his own former employer. And sagging visitor numbers at Barefoot Caverns. Not to mention directing the small staff that ensured that local roads were kept clear of snow and that the water mains were kept from freezing solid.

But events had moved the farm up to the top of the list.

For thirty-seven years, Dad poured his sweat and affection into those ten acres of Christmas trees. And during those years, the extra money had helped keep the family afloat through some lean times. But for the past few years, times had been extra lean. Everything his dad owned was mortgaged to the hilt—all the equity lines used to pay the medical bills Marc's wife left behind after her passing.

Marc's finances weren't much better. He had been a worker at the Blue Moon before the mine went belly-up—given only a minuscule monthly stipend and three months of severance. No financial institution on earth would loan an out-of-work miner with no prospects the $35,000 required to save his father's Christmas tree farm from a tax-lien auction.

The land was a family legacy. His five-times great-grandparents had owned it and passed it down. Bob and Betty Greathouse used it to grow the food they served at Plum's. Even though they sold the plot to Marc's dad many years ago, they still kept their gardens and greenhouses on the property, on the outskirts of the Christmas trees. Generations of Greathouses had tilled and worked this land.

The idea of losing the farm filled Marc with disgust.

Now that it was the first week of December, there were piles of town business to attend to and a growing list of pressing issues. But Marc was ignoring all that. Instead, he was actually preparing to close the mayor's office. For the next several weeks, most of his time would be consumed by doing the same chores he'd spent his youth doing—setting up the warming tent where buyers would indulge in cookies and hot chocolate after traipsing through the snowy "Christmas Forest" to choose a live tree; manning the cashbox; and arranging for carolers.

"Repeatedly explaining to everyone, with a smile, the difference between a Scotch pine and a blue spruce," he said aloud to no one.

It would be the same old drill. He would have to tell every customer, over and over, that yes, *everyone's* tree had to be taller than the eight-foot measuring stick issued at the gates. He would spend the entire Christmas season explaining repeatedly that you could always tag the just-an-inch-too-short tree that your kids had fallen in love with for Christmas *next* year. But not this year. Rules are rules—trees must be eight feet tall, or they don't get cut.

"And no," Marc vented to his empty office, "once your tree has been cut, you cannot decide a tree two rows over is better suited to the ceiling height of your formal living room." From experience, he knew what the next three weeks had in store for him.

Of course, if I want to avoid the whole mess, all I have to do is forget this half-cocked plan, Marc thought, fiddling with the envelope in his hand.

And then it will be my fault. My fault that the farm—which has been in my family for six generations—was sold for pennies on the dollar to some soulless person scouting the county tax lien auction for hard-luck bargains, Marc fumed.

It was truly his dad's fault for failing to pay taxes on the farm for six years—and not telling Marc about it.

And then reality turned his heated indignation for his father into tenderness. His father was aging. Marc refused to use the word *forgetful*. After all, his father had been a deputy for more than forty years, and he still carried a gun in the line of duty. But there were small signs, if a person was looking, of his father's advancing years.

It would be tough, but Marc did have one thing in his favor. It wasn't like there were lots of other places Tippy Canoe residents could go for a tree—it was either the Greathouse farm or drive an hour to Bozeman. Or tramp into the national forest to cut your own tree—after procuring the proper government permit, of course.

Marc still needed to hire local teens to do the actual cutting on the farm. Hiring should have been done weeks ago, not now, more than a week after Thanksgiving. The amount of physical labor involved made it hard to find anyone willing to suffer the job. Administering a level cut with a handsaw often required being prone on the snowy ground. And if sawing one tree required elbow grease, sawing dozens every shift demanded old-fashioned grit. When job applicants learned they'd be in the weather—pelting snow, freezing wind, bitter temperatures—well, plenty of job seekers never showed up for their first day at work.

Truth be told, the daunting task of opening the tree farm a week late, with the townsfolk already clamoring for the trees they have had reserved since before Labor Day weekend, isn't what's really bothering me, Marc admitted. *I've never kept even a small secret from Dad before. And now I'm about to be keeping the granddaddy of all secrets.*

It was a decision so dark it could cost Marc his hard won-mayoral seat—not to mention the tree farm—if anyone ever learned the truth. Marc winced at the thought.

If I don't get the farm open soon, there's no chance of making back the money I need to pay back the money I'm quietly "borrowing" from the city coffers to save the farm.

I'm doing what has to be done, he reminded himself. *And worrying myself into poor health over this won't help. If I follow the plan, by Christmas this will all be over, with no one the wiser. Not a single resident of Tippy Canoe, not even my elderly father—especially not my elderly father—will ever have to know what I'm about to do to keep the tree farm from the threat of a tax lien auction.*

Marc had been over the plan countless times in his mind. The plan would work.

The plan had to work. Failure was unthinkable—seeing the tree farm slip out of the family would crush his father and reverberate through the family tree. Would his grandparents be able to keep Plum's open with their source of food sold to the highest bidder?

I won't have that guilt on my shoulders, he thought. *Better to "borrow" from the city. It's only for a couple weeks, anyway.*

Closing the office, Marc walked across the hall to the post office. Tippy Canoe was a small town, and the city hall had the distinction of not only being a modular building, but also half a modular building. The other half was leased to the US Postal Service for the grand sum of one dollar a year, in exchange for which the town of Tippy Canoe got its own Post Office, open one day each week—Tuesdays—for the business of buying stamps and weighing packages.

At least I didn't have to go far to commit this crime, Marc thought. But his attempt to lighten his own mood failed—the joke wasn't really funny. *I don't want to do this*, he thought, *and that's the truth.*

Since the moment a week ago that his father had broken down and admitted to Marc that the farm was about to be sold at auction to settle unpaid taxes, Marc had been unable to see any other way to get the money.

"This is just a stopgap," he said aloud to no one. "I will have it all paid back—with a generous interest—before the New Year."

He had to do it.

He hesitated a moment longer. And then, with a sigh and a heavy heart, he slipped the envelope with a $35,000 check inside into the mail slot.

The deed was done.

Now everything depends on my ability to squeeze a payday from the Christmas tree farm. A quick, $35,000 payday.

6

At the hotel that evening, Hallie was restless, her mind uneasy. So she did the only sensible thing and ordered room service—opting for the butter-Parmesan fettuccine off the menu. Everyone in this town must know how to cook, because the pasta was warm and sinfully rich. Plus the waiter who delivered it even ground fresh black pepper over the noodles to suit her taste. Served with a side of Caesar salad, the pasta put Hallie in her happy place.

After the meal, she intended to head to bed early, relaxing with *Bleak House*. She adored Dickens, having fallen in love with his novels when she was a girl. If pressed, she would say her favorites were *Hard Times* and *The Old Curiosity Shop*. Come to think of it, it was all a bit ironic. She was having hard times with a curious little shop. And *Bleak House* was a novel about the unintended consequences of trying to settle an estate. Hopefully, her troubles wouldn't be nearly as dramatic.

After fluffing her pillows and settling in to read for a while, Hallie found she just couldn't get into the story. Her mind wouldn't stop turning over all the business of the day. Things did not look promising for either the trading company or the rented storefronts.

She could hear the pitch she would give to a possible buyer: *This property is a steal, especially if you own hungry horses and like pizza and dessert.* Somehow, she didn't think that was going to fly. But what choice did she have? She couldn't stay here, for heaven's sake.

For one, she wasn't a businesswoman. So far, her only exposure to the business world had been in dealing with the commissions taken by the galleries representing her work in Los Angeles, New York, and Italy.

For another, she didn't belong here in the middle of snow and absolutely nowhere. She was a big-city kind of girl. Now Venice, that was more her speed.

Recently, Hallie's work had unexpectedly caught the eye of the curators from the Peggy Guggenheim Collection, which was housed in the famous widow's Grand Canal mansion, Palazzo Venier dei Leoni. The museum had mounted a year long exhibition of her paintings—a rare honor for a living artist. Hallie had lived in the artist-in-residence quarters of the huge palazzo during that year. The experience of living on the Venetian Grand Canal had been one of the highlights of her artistic journey so far, and of her life in general. The beauty and elegance of all the old world surroundings had kicked her creative juices into overdrive and inspired her latest work. Bringing her signature primitive style to a Venetian theme had her gallery representatives salivating— original Venetian art always commanded a premium price.

She had been in the final weeks of defining the scope of the series when the call came informing her that she was now the owner of a small business in some tiny Montana backwater.

Hallie sighed.

Reluctantly, she admitted that the urgent call to come to Montana had actually worked out well, despite her initial hesitation. She had come to a point in the Venetian series where she needed to step away, to get some distance from her art so that she could view it with a fresh perspective. Taking this week or two away from the studio would give her that chance and allow her to see the paintings with fresh eyes when she returned.

Still, she didn't want to be away from the studio too long, didn't want to lose the thread of the perspective she had been creating. She only allowed herself the break on the condition that she would come here, dispose of Finn's estate, and maybe spend a few days taking a snow-coach tour in Yellowstone National Park. It would be hard to pass up an opportunity to see such amazing views while she was this close. But then it was straight home to her studio with—hopefully—a renewed critical eye.

Hallie closed the book after realizing she had been on the same page for ten minutes. There was no way she was going to be able to slow her internal motor enough to relax. Hmmm. It was only ten o'clock. The rock shop, pizzeria, and ice cream parlor would be closed. There hadn't been a chance to examine the properties—her properties—in detail. And she had not so much as opened the door to Finn's Kobold Trading Company. If she went back now, she'd have a chance to look things over alone, in peace.

Her self-guided, late-night tour of Kobold's Trading Company didn't reveal any immediate surprises. Chock-full of tourist fare, the shop carried something for every taste. Oddly enough, there were no stuffed moose or anything else moose-ish in the whole store. Maybe Finn kept a little piece of her in mind when he stocked his store. Not likely, but it was a nice thought.

After exploring the shelves and displays at the back of the store, she found a decrepit, narrow staircase leading down to a wooden door. It was adorned with an intricate arts-and-crafts-style back plate in brass and a blown-glass knob. Everything about the door seemed to be original. Hallie traced the cool metal of the back plate with her finger and felt the smooth, solid knob of blue-green glass. It took her breath away to find such an unexpected beauty. What other vintage treasures might be hiding behind the door? Only one way to find out.

The door was unlocked and opened easily. The smell of dank cement and old wood met her nose. Just inside the door was a light switch. When she flipped it on, several bare bulbs dimly lit a cavernous basement, partially divided into sections, each opening onto the next. Hallie gathered that the basement had apparently been a living space at one time, though it was clear from the general disarray that it was now used as inventory storage for the four storefronts above.

From somewhere in the back of the basement, she heard a soft whiffling sound. Maybe a cranky, old radiator or boiler for heat.

Between stacks of cardboard boxes, Hallie could see the floor was covered with an ancient, floral-patterned wool carpet, like straight out of somebody's granny's house. But the wood accents were fantastic. The room was trimmed in mahogany, and built-in bookcases with leaded-glass panes jutted from the walls.

Beyond the bookcases, the middle of the large basement was defined by a long, shallow, farm-kitchen sink. A wood table shoved up against the wall was strewn with soda cans, pizza boxes, and empty bags of chips. The whole place could use a good cleaning.

She could still hear the gentle noise at the back of the room, almost a low whistle. The pattern of the sound was erratic.

The third section of the basement—beneath Tumpi's Pizzeria?—had once been partitioned off by a curtain of thick cloth strung along a wire pulley. Drawn open and rotting in place, the curtains clearly hadn't been touched in years. Except by moths.

In the corner was a door, ajar. Probably a bathroom. It was from this room that the low noise was coming. She was going to have to investigate.

The door creaked grumpily when she peered in. As her eyes adjusted to the shadows, she could see it was actually an old darkroom. Someone had once processed film into photographs here. Her mother used to have a darkroom in her own basement, years ago. In fact, that was one of the reasons she became in interested in art in the first place

As Hallie scanned the room, she made out two lengths of fabric laid out across the floor. She wondered if the damp air would damage it. Perhaps she should pick it up, whatever it was, and put it somewhere safer.

Stepping closer, she realized it wasn't fabric lengths at all, but two thin sleeping bags laid on low cots.

And the wiffling wasn't a boiler.

Someone was snoring

One of the bags moved. And then the other.

Hallie had a moment's thought that this was like a reverse fairy tale—with the bears waking up in Goldilocks's house.

Two men bolted upright, their hair wild, their faces unshaven. Even as Hallie backed away, they bounded clumsily out of the sleeping bags—getting tangled up in their red long underwear—clearly startled to find they were no longer alone.

"Every mutt does strut with a big donut!" stammered one of the men in a loud and panicked voice. His eyes moved around the room wildly.

"Price cut, boil gut, spending glut, scuttlebutt," blurted the second man, his voice alarmed. His movements were disjointed and frantic.

Hallie shrieked, hitting a pitch that would have made any opera singer proud. Then she took off.

As she fled, the two men began rattling off nonsensical rhymes even louder. She flew up the basement stairs, through the store, and out to the street. Hopefully they weren't following her, but she wasn't about to turn around and find out. Her continuing screams started a flurry of panic by the handful of evening customers coming and going from Plum's Pantry.

Flinging open the door to the restaurant, Hallie hollered, "Call 9-1-1! Get the police!"

"I'll call the deputies." One of the waitresses rushed to a phone.

The diners stopped eating in light of the commotion, and several rallied around Hallie.

"Are you hurt?"

"Did someone attack you?"

"Were you robbed?"

Hallie sank bonelessly into a chair. "Homeless," she gasped, struggling to calm her heaving chest. She hadn't run that far or that fast in years. She swore to start jogging on the beach when she got back home. "There are vagrants. Sleeping. In the basement. Over there." She flung her arm tiredly in the direction across the street.

The waitress repeated Hallie's words into the phone. "Which shop? The dispatcher wants to know—which shop?"

"Kobold," gasped Hallie. "Trading Company."

The waitress repeated the name into the receiver. "Dispatch wants to know if it's the Deans. Did someone hurt the Dean twins? Are they okay?"

The clutch of people surrounding Hallie erupted with concern. Had the Deans been attacked? Was there an intruder? Did the Deans need help?

Did they *need help?* Hallie thought incredulously. *What about me?*

Most of the crowd ran from the restaurant, heading to Kobold's, leaving Hallie to fend for herself.

Someone handed Hallie a glass of water, which she drank gratefully, wishing that *something* in this backward town made sense.

7

"Lyman and Lehman Dean," explained Plum's Pantry-owner Betty Greathouse gently. "They're twins—the sons of Barb Fenton, who has worked here in our restaurant forever. Her sons have a form of autism."

Of course they would be related to Barb, Hallie thought.

There was now a clutch of people loitering in Plum's Pantry, trying to make heads or tails of what the commotion was about.

"We're a small town, and we take care of our own out of duty and necessity," Bob Greathouse said, sitting down next to his wife. "They are local sons. It's not the way it would be done in Los Angeles, I'm sure, but it's the way we do it in Tippy Canoe."

"Not to mention they are family." Betty reached over to grasp Bob's hand. "Barb is Bob's first cousin."

"The Deans are sort of a town project," Melora offered, popping up out of nowhere. Where she had come from, Hallie didn't know. Probably the super speedy gossip mill or phone tree at work.

The brothers are harmless, explained the friendly faces surrounding Hallie. And inseparable, keeping to themselves and living as quasi-hermits for years.

"They've spoken in rhyme since they learned to talk, probably because of the autism. When they're not speaking in rhymes, they both have difficulty with stuttering. They tend to greet anyone who speaks to them with variations of the same nonsensical rhyme, always having to do with donuts," Betty added.

"Retards should have been put in a home years ago if you ask me. Mixed nuts are a public nuisance," a man said from the next booth over. He was wearing worn coveralls with grease stains and a brand new mustard stain from the hamburger hovering next to his lips between bites.

Hallie winced.

The serene look vanished from Betty's face. "Kenny, I think you wanted that food to go, didn't you?" Betty waved the server over. "Staci, please box up the rest of Mr. Petrolo's food before he makes himself even more unwelcome."

Betty turned back toward Hallie, her forehead still drawn with anger. Hallie made a mental note not to tick off Grandma Greathouse.

"The boys have been on their own for a while now. They were close to their father until he died, ten years ago," Bob said, bringing the conversation back on track. "They have never had the same connection with their mother, Barb. Since their father died, everyone has kind of kept an eye out for them, and everyone lends them a hand if they need it."

"Andrea Linford, the woman you ran—er, the woman who slid into you—who owns the weekly paper, she hires them," Melora said, wincing slightly at her slip. "They love basketball, and during game season they write up all the local high school games for the paper. It's their only job, really."

Hallie ignored the tick in her eye at the "ran over" implication. The history lesson did make her feel a little better. Most of all, she was glad the men weren't drug addicts or escaped convicts or something. But that still didn't explain what they were doing in her basement.

"As your attorney, I should have mentioned the Deans and their—" Bob Greathouse paused. "Unusual living arrangement. Christiansen's is your building now. Truthfully . . ." He shrugged his shoulders sheepishly. "I had forgotten about them," he said, color rising to his cheeks. "They keep to themselves. They don't socialize much."

How on earth could anyone forget those two?

"Years ago, when they first left home and started spending more time in the forest, Finn's father found them asleep in the basement of Christiansen's one sub-zero winter night," Bob said. "He gave them some food and a key. They've spent some time there every winter since, and Finn let that continue after his father died."

"Everyone in town just sort of knows that in the dead of winter, the twins can usually be found there after dark," Melora said.

"It's been a great comfort to Barb through these years to know her sons had a warm place." Betty reached across the table to grab Hallie's hand.

Silence fell across the group.

Slowly, Hallie realized that everyone was looking at her expectantly. Now she knew why they were telling her all this. The unspoken message was clear: they were asking her, as the new owner, to honor the arrangement.

This just keeps getting better and better, she thought sarcastically. *If you weren't dead already, Finn, I'd wring your neck.*

By the time Lieutenant Damon Oster and his partner, Lyle Greathouse—who introduced himself as Bob and Betty's son and the mayor's father—had arrived at Kobold's, there were already two dozen people in the basement trying to calm the Dean brothers. Lieutenant Oster said they were understandably rattled after being woken up from their slumber on the floor of the darkroom by a stranger—a woman who ran away screaming, no less.

They were rattled, Hallie snorted to herself. *I was the one scared senseless by two lumbering creatures that looked and sounded like they came straight out of a Dr. Seuss book.*

For the second night in a row, Hallie had unwittingly harmed a beloved local. And though neither incident was her fault, she felt terrible about both. Even so, she was in no hurry to meet the twins again or to try to explain to anyone that she meant no harm. Probably wouldn't do a lot of good anyway. She was not only going be known as the woman who ran over Andrea but also as the witch that scared the life out of those simple twins. Best to let the locals tend to their own.

While the others were busy, Melora sat with Hallie in the restaurant, chatting away about the other jobs the Deans had been doing for years to earn a little spending money. One was rock-hounding for geodes, quartz crystals, topaz, fossils, and any other unusual or interesting mineral. They carted these into town every few months to sell to David and Melora, who retailed them in Cracked Rock.

It was obvious from the extended list of things the two men worked on that the whole town had a hand in making sure that they were taken care of.

Clearly, any change that meant the Deans would no longer be welcome to sleep in the basement of Christiansen's was simply out of the question. Yet another reason to sell the place to one of the locals and be done with the whole mess.

The voice on the phone was unfamiliar. "Is this Mayor Marc Greathouse, of Tippy Canoe Township?" the man asked a second time.

"That's me." Marc wondered what emergency—or more likely, non-emergency that someone felt was an emergency—he was being called upon to solve. The job of being a small-town mayor was thankless and never-ending. And he had a Christmas tree farm to open.

"This is Tim Brotherton of the *Bozeman Daily Chronicle*, calling to ask a few questions about the governor's press conference out there this afternoon."

"Press conference?" Marc laughed out loud. "I think you've got the wrong mayor on the horn. This is the mayor of Tippy Canoe you're talking to. Most of the time, Governor Tidewater tries to pretend we don't exist. He couldn't come up with enough guts to show up out here for some glad-handing press conference. We're not exactly big supporters around here, if you know what I mean." A three-term governor, Tidewater had a long history of ignoring the needs of the state's most rural outposts. Standing up to Tidewater and his irresponsible policies had been one of the things that got Marc elected as mayor. It was also one of the things that kept him on the governor's radar.

There was a long silence on the line. "So this is Mayor Greathouse? Tippy Canoe's mayor?

"Is this a prank call?" Marc, like most small-town residents, didn't suffer fools gladly. "I'm not in the mood. I've got a Christmas tree farm that needed to be open yesterday."

"This is not a prank call," the voice said. "We just want to know how you plan to respond to Governor Tidewater's announcement that he will shut down Tippy Canoe Academy because of the statewide budget crisis."

"Gall-durn-it, I don't have time for jokes, son," Marc said gruffly, realizing he actually sounded like his own father in that moment. "I'm going to hang up now, and when I do, I hope you'll get yourself a life."

"This is not a joke, sir. This is an interview request. From Tim Brotherton of the *Bozeman Daily Chronicle*."

Something about the tone of the young man's voice convinced Marc to stay on the line.

After finishing the call from the journalist, the first thing Marc did was call the governor's office in Helena.

"We sent you an email last week," an exasperated staffer said in reply. "Perhaps your staff misplaced it or neglected to direct your attention to it."

"I *am* my staff. This is Tippy Canoe Township. I'm the secretary, the janitor, the town punching bag. I'm the whole shebang." Marc's voice was rising. "And I have a tree farm to manage, an aging father to keep an eye on, grandparents to keep in business, not to mention our own local budget crisis to attend to, and a municipally owned cave to manage. Please excuse me if I'm a little behind on my email."

"Uh-huh," the flunky from the governor's office said.

Marc decided to get to the point. "So it's true?"

"Well, yes. Governor Tidewater will be there—at Tippy Canoe Township, that is—at three o'clock to address his plan for proactively addressing the state education budget deficit."

"He's coming to close our school."

"This is an opportunity for your youth to participate in programs they would not otherwise have access—"

"He's coming to close our school. As in, shut it down."

The voice in the phone sighed. "We are offering your students—"

"Don't tell me this is another attempt to revive the asinine plan to bus our kids out of Sweet Grass County and over to Meagher County."

"Sir, the state budget—"

"And you sneaky suckers sent an email, hoping no one out here would notice that you were shutting down our school." Marc knew he was unfairly letting this flunky have the brunt of his anger. But this idiot probably got paid four times Marc's minuscule salary and sat in a cushy office all day to boot.

"As I tried to explain, sir, the state budget—"

Marc slammed down the phone.

Marc's afternoon became a flurry of phone calls and go-nowhere conversations, all leading to the same conclusion: the state was in a bind, money-wise, and Tidewater was up for re-election. In a show of campaign zeal, the governor was bending to the state's more populated areas, where there was hollering about a lack of education spending. Tidewater would be announcing his proposal to close a dozen or so so-called "pioneer schools" that still operated in the smallest towns in Montana. Tidewater needed to give the state's biggest school districts more money or risk the ire of the voters.

"Consolidating" Tippy Canoe's tiny, one-school district into the neighboring county would free up valuable taxpayer dollars to be used in other more important districts, Marc was told by someone in the state's education office.

"Never mind that Tippy Canoe Academy is living history," Marc shot back. Not to mention that it had one of the highest per-student grade-point averages in the state. Or that the school's fabled marching band program had won countless coveted national titles in competition, outperforming every other music program in Montana by far. But his protests were only greeted with dial tones.

Statewide media, including television crews, newspaper journalists, and radio talk show pundits, had begun arriving in Tippy Canoe an hour before, all wanting a statement from the mayor. Far from completing the last-minute work necessary for opening the tree farm, Marc found himself stuck in his office—which was supposed to be closed.

As promised, Governor Hyrum Tidewater arrived at 3:00 p.m., pulling up in an unmarked, black Cadillac Escalade and followed by a second unmarked, black Escalade. The moment the vehicles stopped, staffers jumped out and scanned the scene, and within two minutes they had a podium bearing the state seal set up with a microphone and portable speakers. Former Tippy Canoe-er, smarmy Dickie Hatch, the governor's lapdog, appeared to be heading the charge.

Ten minutes later, Governor Tidewater was grandstanding in an attempt to garner support for his latest spending proposal he would send to the school board.

As always, thought Marc, *Tidewater knows how to milk the last ounce of drama out of any opportunity to plant himself in front of the television cameras—and thus the voters*. At the moment, Tidewater was raising his fists in defiance of a state budget deficit he himself had created.

"And so, I stand here today to take a stand for fiscal responsibility," Tidewater continued, to minor applause from the crowd gathered. *Mostly his own staffers, Escalade'd in at taxpayer expense,* Marc noted irately.

"Closing this school," Tidewater gestured to the building behind him, "and small schools like it around the great state of Montana would allow your education tax dollars to be spent more effectively. Why, consolidating this"—he hurriedly checked his notes—"Tippy Academy"—an aide standing behind him whispered in his ear—"er, Tippy Canoe Academy, that is, would free up enough money to fund the free school lunch program in Montana's four largest counties."

Marc noted the governor's girth. Tidewater didn't appear to have missed too many chimes of the dinner bell at the governor's mansion. He wondered what portion of the budget Tidewater spent each year on fancy, official state dinners.

"Any questions?" Tidewater, looking triumphant, asked the media horde.

"Yes," Marc hollered from the crowd. He was about to broach the boundaries of polite behavior. But as his father often said, playing polite is rarely the same as doing right—progress comes when you question the bums in office. Marc noted his father, dressed in his official deputy uniform—a formality he rarely bothered with these days when on duty—and his partner, Lieutenant Damon Oster, were standing behind Tidewater on the steps of Tippy Canoe Academy. Was his father simply rising to the occasion on behalf of Tippy Canoe, or had Tidewater's office actually ordered him to show up to make the whole presentation look more official—and dramatic, Marc wondered.

"Yeah, I have a question," Marc repeated, glaring at Tidewater, who was glancing around trying not to notice him. "Marc Greathouse, mayor of Tippy Canoe, and local voting precinct chairman." He threw that at the old goat, just to remind Tidewater that he still answered to the voters, even in Tippy Canoe. "Why is it that, until a few hours ago, no one from your office, or any office for that matter, had bothered to tell anyone here in Tippy

Canoe—including me, the mayor—that you had blithely decided to do away with our historic pioneer school?"

Tidewater didn't miss a beat. "As your governor of the great state of Montana, I am charged with making the hard decisions. The whole state is hurting. Everyone is making sacrifices. Cuts have to be made."

"How much have you cut your salary and expense account?" Marc knew he was being small. But criminy, Tidewater was soulless, pushing to shut down the Academy with nothing to offer but canned talking points exclaimed in the pseudo-heroic voice that passes for leadership these days. "I suppose it's no coincidence that you didn't carry the majority vote in Tippy Canoe. Political retribution—just another day of business as usual."

"Pay attention, Mr. Mayor," hissed Tidewater, putting his hand over the microphone. "What we're talking about here is something bigger than your podunk *Tipsy* Canoe cry-babying."

The crowd went silent. "Tipsy Canoe" was a derogatory term used to put down Tippy Canoe residents, a historic slur painting Tippy Canoe-ers as drunks, listless, and useless.

"You repugnant, slack-jawed politician," Marc spat, launching himself toward the governor. And before anyone could move to stop him, the mayor of "Tipsy Canoe" popped the governor of the great state of Montana square in the nose.

In front of a bank of television cameras and journalists.

The melee that erupted lasted several minutes. Marc was wrestled to the ground by Dickie Hatch and another unnamed government goon, prompting some of the local residents—also no friends of Tidewater—to grab those who had grabbed Marc.

A brawl broke out, and the media ate it up, cameras rolling.

Several long minutes passed before Deputy Greathouse and Lieutenant Oster got some semblance of control of the crowd. "Now hold up just a minute," Oster shouted. "I said hold up, now! Just let's get a look at ourselves. This isn't the way to act, no matter how we, er, *you* feel about the governor and his politics. Keep it up, and I'm going to have to arrest the lot of you for inciting a riot."

"Well," Tidewater said, dusting himself off and using his pocket handkerchief to dab the slow, bloody drip from his nose. "Do your duty, officers."

Taken aback, Greathouse and Oster just stared at the governor.

"Arrest him," Tidewater said, pointing to Marc. "He assaulted a sitting governor. Arrest him."

Deputy Greathouse looked from the governor, to his son, to Lieutenant Oster, and back to the governor.

"I said, *arrest him.*"

Both Greathouse and Oster looked thunderstruck and uncomfortable with the position they found themselves in.

"Oh, go on, Dad," Marc said. "Handcuff me. I got him square in the nose, after all. I'm not looking for any favors."

"I'll be darned—he's your dad." The governor snorted a laugh. "Well, go on. Cuff your loudmouth son. No favoritism, now. Do your duty to the law, deputy."

Moving mechanically, Deputy Greathouse did as he was ordered. When the handcuffs were in place, Tidewater sidled up to Marc, speaking just low enough so only Marc could hear. "Arrested by your own pa. This backwater's more backward than I'd heard. But hear this . . . there will be repercussions for this little stunt. Both for your beloved *Tipsy* Canoe and for you personally."

9

Flash was well known for his brilliant ideas. At least that's why he chose the nickname for himself: always thinking up stuff in a flash. That and a preoccupation in younger days with flash-bombing mailboxes

Pacing back and forth, he knew one thing for sure: he needed one of those ideas now. No way would he stand by, helpless, while a fortune—millions of dollars, at least—slipped through his fingers.

Never in my life has heaven seen fit to tempt me with money, he thought, remembering the old Broadway tune, "If I Were a Rich Man," that had kindled his childhood imagination.

Now it had all landed right in his lap. Finally, people would give him the respect he was due. He was destined for this.

Or would have been, if Mayor Smarty Pants hadn't gotten in the way. He was this close to making it all happen. To pulling off the deal of the century, right under everybody's noses. But that wasn't going to happen anymore, and all because some Boy Scout mayor of flea-bitten Tippy Canoe, Montana, couldn't keep his nose to his own business. No, the high-horse mayor just had to go and try to save the day again. But he wasn't going to give up that easily. No one could stand in the way of fate. All he needed was a plan.

10

At the front desk, the clerk at Hotel Speleo handed Hallie a message: Andrea Linford, who was home from the hospital and recovering from her broken leg, wondered if Hallie would stop by her house for a visit.

No way. Was this lady serious? Hallie didn't know what to make of the invitation, but she was wary. In her experience, everyone was always looking out for number one, trying to get ahead. Meeting Andrea might be a mistake . . . a trap lying in wait. But she could hardly refuse to visit the woman she had run over. Could she?

Andrea Linford's home sat on the corner of a tree-lined avenue just blocks from Tippy Canoe's Main Street business district. A large porch wrapped the home and overlooked an extensive rose garden.

A young woman answered the door. Introducing herself as Megan, Andrea's daughter, she showed Hallie to a sunroom at the back of the house. Shutting the door behind her, Megan left Hallie and Andrea alone.

"I was hoping you would come," Andrea said with a smile,

motioning Hallie to sit in an oversized, white wicker chair next to her raised and cast laden leg. "I had to tell you thank you."

"Thank you . . . for getting into an accident," Hallie said, carefully choosing her words so as not to incriminate herself. She couldn't resist looking around the room for a hidden camera. Journalists were known for using sneaky tactics to catch people on tape.

Andrea seemed genuine enough and leaned toward Hallie, lowering her voice. "You've changed my daughter's life. Oh, it's been wonderful. A true godsend!"

Hallie wondered what kind of pain medication this woman was on—and how much.

Two years ago, Andrea explained, her daughter, Megan, had had her learner's driving permit. She had been weeks away from taking her driving test and getting her license. Then Andrea's late husband, Dale, had suffered a heart attack while driving, coincidentally, at the same intersection where Andrea had slid into Hallie's rented SUV.

"After Dale died, both Megan and I couldn't bring ourselves to get back behind the wheel of a car," Andrea said. "For a while, we walked most everywhere or got a ride with friends who understood we needed time. This summer, I started riding my bike a lot, going to work and back, shopping, things like that. When winter temperatures hit, I still couldn't get up enough courage to drive the car—especially because Dale's accident, well, it happened in the snow on the icy road."

Voice breaking, Andrea paused in her storytelling, as if reliving her own private nightmares. When she finally continued, her tone was stronger and less emotional. "Just recently, I'd seen something on television or read somewhere about the growing popularity of motor scooters, especially with the price of gas always seeming to be on the rise. The salesman told me that if I could ride a bike, I could manage a motor scooter without any problems—those were his exact words. 'Without any problems,' " Andrea said. "So

I bought the darn thing. I even took it for a test drive around the block with the salesman, and it felt good—liberating, even. Somehow, in my mind it seemed so much safer than a car—really funny, knowing what I know now, of course."

The night Hallie had arrived in town, Andrea had realized she needed a few groceries for breakfast, she explained.

"Milk, eggs, ice cream, who can remember," Andrea continued. "I told Megan I'd just zip over to the grocery store on my new scooter. Five blocks was all I had to go. Next thing Megan knows, my friend Barb is knocking on the door saying that I've been taken to the hospital in Bozeman by ambulance."

She paused. "At first, I was really mad at myself for letting this happen. But since my leg's been broken, Megan has had to drive me home from the hospital and to my doctor's appointments and do the grocery shopping—and that's just in the past three days. For the first time since her father died, she's driving again."

Tears gathered in Andrea's eyes

"Forgive me; I am on a lot of pain medication, as you have probably gathered. I'm not normally this emotional in front of people I don't know. I'll tell you a secret: I think this was all supposed to happen. It's too much of a coincidence—me having my accident at the same intersection where my husband was killed."

She leaned in and began to whisper. "I haven't told Megan this yet. But I think this was Dale's way of telling me that he's okay, and that both Meg and I need to get back to living our lives. I don't know if that makes any sense to you, but it feels right to me. " She laughed, straightening herself. "Of course, buying the motor scooter felt right to me too! Maybe I'm just crazy. Or a glutton for punishment."

Hallie was leaning toward the side of crazy. It was definitely out there to think that the spirit of your dead husband would want you to get in an accident so that you could move on. But who was she to judge? They say that there are more things in heaven and earth after all. And just in case there was actually anything to this, Hallie sent up a quick prayer to Finn, if he was listening—no accidents to give her a message, please.

Hallie was touched that, despite the circumstances of their initial meeting, Andrea had reached out to her in friendship. She hesitantly decided to reach back. "Why haven't you told your daughter about how you feel? Perhaps it's something she needs to hear."

A thoughtful look lit Andrea's face. "You know, you're right. It's just, well, this feels special to me. Maybe *sacred* is the word. I don't know if you have adult children, but Meg is nineteen years old. If I told her that I think her father arranged for me to break my leg under your SUV so Megan would start driving again, well, she might call for the men in white coats to haul me off to a rubber room."

Andrea laughed, and Hallie found herself laughing with her. There was something about this woman that Hallie just couldn't help liking. The two women shared a smile. It was completely bizarre to Hallie that she would be here, sharing personal feelings with a woman that just a few days ago had basically accused her of attempted murder by Yukon. But Hallie was getting used to stepping through the looking glass in this town, and this time she decided to go with it and accept the growing friendship.

An hour later, the two women were chatting away like old friends.

"I understand our little accident also introduced you to our handsome and single mayor—probably not what you had expected for your first moments in town." Andrea winked.

Hallie told Andrea how Marc helped her amid the shock and panic over the accident, and then how she met him again the next day at Plum's Pantry.

"He's had it rough these past few years," Andrea said, preparing to launch into backstory, as all the locals seemed prone to do for one another.

This time though, Hallie was all ears.

"Kathlyn, his wife. She died—oh, what's it been?—probably over three years ago now. Breast cancer, a really bad case. She had a terrible struggle with it, and she fought until the very end. Marc was not the same after he lost her. You can imagine."

"I've lost a couple of friends to breast cancer. It can be brutal," Hallie said knowingly. "Did they have children?"

"Never had children. They married awfully young. Probably thought they had time, but then there was the sickness and all. He had his hands full taking care of her and working full time at the Blue Moon Mine."

Hallie was going to ask more questions about the handsome civil servant, but Andrea jumped in before she had the chance.

"Speaking of the Blue Moon, I have to admit there is a second reason why I invited you here," Andrea said finally, her tone a little mischievous.

"Ah-ha," Hallie said, her guard rising a little. She felt sure that she was about to hear the catch for this friendliness. "Let me preface by saying that I don't know what your plans are," Andrea started. "But whether you intend to sell Christiansen's or have someone local manage the business for you, I thought you might want to know what you're up against."

"Thank you," Hallie said, unsure exactly what the words *up against* referred to. "I'd be glad for any inside information you'll give me."

According to Andrea, for more than a century, Tippy Canoe had existed mainly because of the Blue Moon Silver Mine. As far back as anyone could remember, the mine had had a contract with the largest manufacturers of photographic paper. The mine had provided the raw silver needed to make the silver gelatin necessary for developing prints of film for cameras.

"Then the digital camera came along, and the mine owners had a hard time finding new contracts for their silver. Probably a combination of bad business dealings and dwindling silver recovery. But when the last film company stopped buying silver, the Blue Moon had finally met its match, so to speak."

"More than half the residents worked there, and with it finally going belly-up, everybody's hurtin'." Andrea sighed. "We're all struggling to survive on tourism to the cave."

The idea that a little digital camera would have such a ripple effect and wreak havoc on so many hard-working people's lives was mind-boggling. "I'm guessing there hasn't been much call for a digital-camera store in town," Hallie said, hoping to lighten the mood a bit.

"We've all got them," Andrea said with a chuckle. "Just like the rest of the world. You can't pretend change isn't happening. You have to adapt. Darwin and all that."

Since the mine had started laying off people over the last few years, local business leaders—Andrea included, of course—had created an alliance, hoping that by working together, they could find ways to encourage more tourists.

"Whether you like it or not, right now, you're one of the largest commercial landlords in our little town," Andrea said. "And you have a fresh, outsider's perspective. We've all lived here so long that sometimes I wonder whether we can see past tradition—you know, the inertia of being comfortable in our routines—to the possibilities for positive change. It would mean a lot to us if you could come to our next meeting. It would mean a lot to me personally, for whatever that's worth."

The request caught Hallie off guard. She felt for the little town, but she was only in town for the week. Two weeks at most. What on earth could she do to help? "I haven't even toured the cave," she stammered. "If I'm being honest, I didn't even know there was a cave in Tippy Canoe until I arrived. I'm not sure I'd have much to offer."

"I'll arrange a special tour for you," Andrea said. And then before Hallie could object, Andrea added, "You'll want to tour Barefoot before you leave town anyway. I'll make sure you get a private tour with the best guide. And it's a breathtaking work of natural art. You have to see to believe."

"I have to go *barefoot?*" Hallie asked incredulously, still stuck on the first part of Andrea's speech. No wonder the town had tourist issues if the tourists had to take off their shoes to go into a cave.

Andrea rolled her eyes. "No, city girl. You wear hiking boots. The name of the cave is Barefoot Caverns."

Oh. That explained a lot. Still, Hallie didn't own a pair of hiking boots. But before she could speak, Andrea pressed on.

"Seeing the cave in person will give you a perspective on how we might be able to boost tourism to save our downtown businesses. Meeting with our alliance members would be an opportunity for you to meet the rest of the business owners, and vice versa. I have a hunch that you intend to either sell the place or find a manager. Either way, your best bets are going to be the business owners at the meeting tomorrow. So you see"—Andrea paused, a mischievous gleam in her eye—"it's really in your best interest to come to our little shindig. Thanks to the rotten economy, all we business folk are in the same boat. The same tippy canoe, you could say."

11

We're going to stage a press conference of our own."

Privately, Marc Greathouse might have considered Ula Blackboro to be Tippy Canoe's busiest old-biddy busybody. But at this moment, he'd never been so happy to see her deeply wrinkled face.

"I was coming here to bail you out," Ula said in her usual, unduly loud voice. "But instead of plunkin' down my hard-earned cash for your freedom, I guess I get to be the bearer of good news. Our *great* governor has had a last-minute change of heart. More likely, he's looking to come off as the mercy-minded victim to the media. Anyway," she harrumphed, "he's ordered the deputies to let you go. You can still thank me for trying to rescue you. I would have made you pay me back later for the bail money."

"What was the bail?" Marc murmured, not sure he wanted to know the price his own father—who was also Justice of the Peace—had put on his son's head.

"Fifty-five dollars," Ula bleated as though she'd been looking forward to the question. "A mite high, even for the idiot who sucker punched the governor on live television." And then as an afterthought, she added, "He even decreed that you are not a threat to society. Ha!" Her laugh was practically a cackle.

Marc smiled for the first time since he'd been jailed—that is, left to sit alone, on the honor system, in the reservation-only party room at Plum's Pantry. This was because Tippy Canoe had never had a jail. The rare person arrested for a serious crime was usually hauled to the county. The town barely even had an office for Deputy Greathouse and Lieutenant Oster, the town's two part-time—and only—sheriff's deputies. When on the job, Marc's father and his partner used the mayor's desk inside the city hall. The modular had been purchased as temporary space until a real city hall could be built. That had been fifteen years ago.

At age eighty-nine, Ula Blackboro was the oldest resident of Tippy Canoe and had more energy—and certainly more gumption—than most. Nearly thirty years before, she founded "Keepers of the Pioneer Vision." The sole aim of the members of this local club was to keep Tippy Canoe from straying too far from its old-fashioned ways. What that usually meant was keeping things from straying too far from what Ula considered right and honorable.

"I take it you've got a plan." Marc could hardly wait to hear.

"You bet your boot." Ula snickered at the pun on how Barefoot Cavern was discovered. In this town, the pun never got old. At least to some people. "If that miserable excuse for a governor thinks he's going to shut down a historic school that has been providing a fine education to Tippy Canoe residents for *sixteen* consecutive decades, he's up in the night."

"You mentioned a press conference."

"Yeppers."

"Have you ever organized a press conference?"

"No time like the present, I always say."

"I feel certain you have in mind a specific message to convey at this, er, press conference."

"We're going to give that Tidewater a big 'no thanks' to his bumble-along plan to give our historic academy the kiss of death."

And then she added, enigmatically, "The governor may have forgotten his own family roots, but he didn't reckon on Ula Blackboro and the Keepers of the Pioneer Vision."

Marc grinned. Whatever Ula had planned, it was bound to be entertaining.

12

When the lightbulb moment struck, Flash wasn't surprised at his own genius.

Not only would he be able to make his fortune, but there was also an added bonus. He would ruin the Greathouse family all in one fell swoop.

This would be a big job—a bigger job than he could do alone. He'd need help.

And then, another burst of inspiration. He'd need helpers who were hard workers yet dumb as posts. Willing yet reclusive enough to keep mum. Helpers who would work for a song and be happy to do it.

Helpers truly gullible and innocent.

Lyman and Lehman Dean.

He'd met the Deans before through serendipity. Flash had been hanging around near the edge of town, taking care of some business he didn't want anyone to know about. It had been a dusky summer evening, and he'd thought he was alone. But along one of the more deserted stretches, he'd heard a thin, clattering laughter floating from somewhere deep in the lodgepole pine forest beyond the road. Anyone dumb enough to set up camp in the forest obviously had some reason—a recreational substance they didn't want to get caught with. Or share.

He'd crept quietly into the woods, following the wispy sound of almost-derisive snickering. The closer he'd gotten, the harder the noise had been to pinpoint. Eventually, he'd discovered a well-hidden pockmark in the earth, a deep cleft invisible until you nearby stumbled down into it. And at the bottom, some forty or fifty feet below, there had a flickering campfire and the Dean twins.

In this territory, you assume anyone bivouacked in the wildlands is armed. Probably well armed. Best to bide your time before crashing the party. At first, he'd been sure the two men were inebriated at least, if not high. And Flash had wanted in on that action. He'd had some cash. That was usually enough for an invitation, if not a warm welcome.

But the longer he'd observed the two men, the more puzzled he'd become. Something was off. They'd chattered random, silly phrases in chirping voices, often stammering, laughing all the while. And without warning—often midsentence—they would fall silent, as if they had plunged into the rabbit hole, vanishing from reality into their own world.

And all this in tandem. The whole thing had been eerie.

Eventually, he had approached them out of boredom. It had been a mistake. The two men had launched into panicked histrionics, bolting for the road, screaming and hollering almost psychotically. The ruckus had drawn attention from the road, and Flash had been hard pressed to convince an impromptu war party that he'd meant the two men no harm.

That night, he'd learned the hard way who the men were—Lyman and Lehman Dean. Twin brothers, autistic and harmless. And not to be bullied. They had no-nonsense allies who, whatever heir personal sins, prided themselves on looking out for the truly humble of the earth.

Being in jail teaches a mayor a thing or two—even if "jail" is really just Plum's, thought Marc.

Maybe twiddling his thumbs in the banquet room had been the first time Marc had an hour to himself to think without someone constantly needing something. Or maybe being arrested by his own father had cleared the cobwebs from his mental processes. Whatever the reason, being in jail had given Marc an epiphany.

He should not have mailed the check.

More to the point, I should not have written the check in the first place, Marc thought.

It was wrong.

He'd known it was wrong, of course. But somehow he'd managed to convince himself that what he'd done wasn't really stealing. Just borrowing. Okay, so technically the money wasn't his. But it was his job to manage it. The account was sitting in the bank unused, just drawing interest, and wouldn't be needed for months, at least.

And when I pay the money back, I'll pay interest. No harm, no foul. It was for the greater good, after all.

At least that had been the plan. But "borrowing" from someone without asking, even if you intend to pay back the money with interest before they ever know it's gone—or even better, without them ever knowing it was gone—well, some people might still think of that as just plain-old, garden-variety stealing.

And stealing could get him sent to a real jail—not an hour in the Plum's Pantry banquet room as a sort of professional courtesy to the governor of Montana.

Marc didn't want to go to jail.

Staring at the aging, purple wallpaper in the banquet room had been terrible enough—and that didn't even involve a strip search, cell mates, or the horrible food. Or lack of privacy. Or steel bars. Or prison uniforms.

Problem was, it was too late for Marc to take back what he'd done. He'd already faxed a photocopy of the check over to the county assessors to halt the auction. But more serious than that, the check was, as they say, in the mail.

From somewhere in the nether reaches of Marc's mind—which admittedly was not as sharp as it had once been in his college days—a memory had surfaced.

He recalled that once upon a time he'd heard or read something about someone sending a letter, and then quickly regretting having put in the mailbox. Something about never acting in your moment of anger, making rash decisions, or writing things you don't really mean. Or at least, when you have a clearer head, things you don't want others to know you'd thought or felt.

The person, whoever they'd been, had taken the wad of wet gum from their own mouth, stuck it onto the end of a pencil, and then eased the contraption into the mailbox to retrieve the letter.

And it had worked. At least in the story Marc had heard. Or read.

Marc ran to the mailbox slot where he'd slipped the letter earlier. The post office was closed today; it was only open for postage sales and weighing packages from noon to five on Tuesdays. His letter had to be in there still. And hopefully, in the day since he had dropped it in, there weren't too many other letters that had been deposited on top of it.

Worth a try, thought Marc. *One way or another, I've got to undo this foolishness.*

If he couldn't get the letter, he could always place a stop-payment order on the check at the bank. But even that might raise suspicion—especially considering the amount the check was written for. And the mere fact that someone might come to know the check existed . . . Well, that alone could be enough to cost Marc everything.

Better to get the check back, before it ever goes out in the mail.

Marc wasn't much of a gum chewer, but he'd found an old piece in his office desk across the hall. He couldn't imagine that a pencil was actually the right tool for sticking through a mail slot to retrieve a letter via sticky wad of gum. But maybe a coat hanger would work. Kind of like the way you used to jimmy a car lock—back in the days before car locks had become electronic.

The entirety of city hall consisted of the mayor's office, a bathroom, a storage room stuffed with filing cabinets, and a tiny closet. Even so, Marc could not find a wire coat hanger. Not in the city hall closet.

He decided to walk two blocks to the cleaners. That way, he'd have time to work over the ancient stick of gum in his mouth.

Confronting the mail-drop slot again, Marc had turned a borrowed wire coat hanger from the cleaners into a length of wire sufficient for mail-drop fishing. Carefully, he applied the wad of gum in such a way that it had a reasonable chance of staying put. He hated to imagine the mess that a wad of gum among Tippy Canoe's mail would cause.

For that matter, Marc thought, *I hate to imagine what would happen if someone walked in here right now and saw me here, with a coat wire in the drop slot.*

Best to work quickly.

Angling the gum down the slot, Marc felt the wire hit something. He gave the wire a press, hoping that if he had actually baited his letter, it would stay stuck to the gum long enough to get it up and through the mail slot. Using a slow, steady motion, he drew the wire up. Through the slot, he could see there was in fact an envelope stuck to the gum. Moving with deliberation, he brought the stuck envelope up to the slot to where he could reach it with his fingers. Then he pulled it through.

It wasn't his.

The letter was from Mrs. Gladys Pickington. Addressed to her son.

And now, it had gum residue on it.

Marc set the envelope on the postal counter. He'd deal with that in a moment. Making sure his gum wad was once again firmly fixed to the coat hanger, he fished again.

This time, he got another Mrs. Gladys Pickington letter. Addressed to her daughter.

Marc guided the wire in for a third attempt. And this time he got back his own letter.

Using nose tissue, he cleaned what he could of the gum residue from Mrs. Pickington's correspondence to her children. The envelopes were each stained where the gum had touched them, but enough tissue had stuck to the residue that Marc felt fairly sure the letters wouldn't gum up the postal sorting machines, so to speak.

In the mayor's office, Marc used the electronic shredder to destroy both the envelope and the check he'd written on "borrowed" funds. He just needed to stop at the bank to transfer the funds back from his personal bank account to the accounts of the Tippy Canoe Township.

That should take care of it. No harm, no fraud, no real jail time.

Except that now he was back where he'd started. The government would notice when his promised check didn't arrive. He'd either have to helplessly watch as the farm was sold at tax auction this weekend, or he'd have to find a better—legal—way to come up with thirty-five thousand dollars.

And fast.

14

Finding the Deans a second time had initially been much harder than Flash bargained for. But when all was said and done, it had been an effort well spent.

He couldn't risk anything as suspicious as openly asking around town if anyone knew where the twins might be. He needed to fly under the radar, try not to be noticed. Their mother, he knew, worked at Plum's Pantry. But marching to the restaurant counter to ask her about the twins was obviously out of the question—assuming she even had a clue where they might be. From what he'd come to understand, the twins were loners, as likely to be nowhere as anywhere you might expect them to be.

But Barb was about the only lead he had. And he was hungry. So he went for a burger and beer. In disguise, since he shouldn't be there.

As it turned out, Lady Fortune was smiling upon him once again—a sure-fire sign that this deal, and the multi-million-dollar payoff he meant to squeeze out of it, were aligned in the stars.

Not five minutes after he'd started in on his bacon cheeseburger and fries, two women came into the café, one with a cast on her leg and using a crutch under her arm.

"Andrea and Megan!" The Deans' mother, Barb, said from behind the counter. She was clearly delighted and surprised. "You must be feeling better if you're up and out of the house! I'm so glad to see you with some color in your cheeks."

Flash listened carefully, making sure to draw no attention to himself. He didn't want to be recognized, just in case. And after fifteen or twenty minutes of gossip . . . jackpot. The conversation rolled around to Barb's sons.

"A yurt? What's a yurt?"

Barb explained that it was a kind of sturdy, circular tent, first used by the ancient nomads. It was weather-tight, and it also held the heat in during winter.

"After that ignorant woman from California scared the bejee-bers out of my boys in the basement of Christiansen's, they've refused to go back," Barb said. "They have that drafty cabin out on the plateau overlooking Dimple Hollow, where they usually spend the summer. But over the past few years, they've spent most of the winter, at Christiansen's. I worried a lot less about them there."

She'd had to do something to find them a new winter home after that horrible woman spooked them. Willful and preferring solitude, the twins had long ago made it clear they weren't going to live with their mother. They preferred the open land, and they knew how to take care of themselves—and each other.

But they were getting older. Winter in a rickety cabin wasn't comfortable or even safe. Lyman and Lehman might deem it ade-quate, but Barb had been beside herself. Local ranchers and hunt-ers had suggested the yurt.

"So I bought one off them. Money-wise, it was a stretch. But I know I'll sleep better on these bitter nights if I know they're sleeping better."

The twins had relished setting up the yurt, and Deputy Greathouse had volunteered to drag the pieces to Dimple Hollow on his snowmobile sled. He'd even kept an eye on the construction and hauled a winter's worth of coal to supply the box stove that came with the yurt kit.

"Lyle even ferried me out there," Barb said with a laugh. "I rode on the back of the snowmobile and spent a night out there with the twins, just to make sure, firsthand, that it was what I had hoped it was. And it's great!"

Bingo. The yurt was about to have a visitor.

15

Marc Greathouse had to admit this much: Ula Blackboro, pain-in-the-patoot that she had been all these many years, might well be an untapped marketing genius.

The town doyenne pulled out all the stops to convince the whiny media to travel all the way back out to Tippy Canoe for a second press conference in as many days. She was billing the event as not only a retaliatory press conference aimed at saving the academy from the governor's clutches, but also as an anti-Tidewater protest demonstration, complete with a burning effigy of the governor himself. And as a tantalizing clue of how the town intended to fight back, they would rename the school, with the new moniker to be revealed at precisely noon, on the school steps.

Apparently, the weeks between Thanksgiving and Christmas were the slowest of slow news days, because the media had descended as a plague of locusts for the second press conference. Ula even called CNN with an underdog-takes-on-powerful-governor pitch. And shockingly, it actually worked. The national cable news channel hired a freelance cameraman to cover the story.

It seemed every resident of Tippy Canoe had turned out with

a protest banner of some sort—even the kids. Wielding posters and pickets, the residents vented their displeasure with old-fashioned protest chants:

"Release your claws from our academy."

"Heck no, our school won't go."

"Cut the pork; impeach the dork."

"Sinking our school is Tidewater's lowest ebb."

"Close the governor's mansion—Keep the academy open."

Even Marc's father—now famous for arresting his own son on live television as the governor looked on—was here, marching the picket line with his fellow Tippy Canoe-ers and holding a protest sign. And once again, he was dressed in his deputy uniform—just in case the irony hadn't already been obvious.

"Bless you, Dad," Marc said aloud with a smile.

All in all, not a bad show, Marc had to admit. Tidewater hadn't taken into account the sting of this nest of unhappy hornets.

From behind Marc, a voice said, "Mayor Greathouse." Marc instantly recognized the voice as belonging to Andrea Linford, owner of the *Creekside Register-Ledger*, the town's weekly paper.

Marc turned around and was surprised to see that Andrea, crutches under her arms, wasn't alone. The pretty new woman was with her—the woman he had met first at the accident and again the next day at Plum's. The one that had occupied his thoughts on and off for the past few days.

"Andrea Linford, don't you know how to rest?" Marc said with a grin. "I'm pretty sure that, many years from now, we'll find you back in your office the day after your funeral, on the job as usual."

Andrea smiled widely. "How could I miss a party like this? I don't think Tippy Canoe has ever seen anything like it."

Marc had to agree with that. He turned to Hallie. "And how is our town's newest business owner today? You probably think we have the governor here once a week. Well, it's true—presidents, governors, heads of state; Tippy Canoe is a hub for the wealthy and powerful of the world. What can we say?" Marc was surprised at the tone of his own voice. Was he openly flirting with this woman? *I am*, he realized. He felt his cheeks color slightly.

"If everyone is greeted personally by the mayor within two minutes of arriving in town, as I was, then I'm not surprised," Hallie said jovially. "Tippy Canoe is nothing if not a beacon of hospitality."

Was she naturally coy and funny, or was she showing interest too? The color crept up to Marc's ears.

At precisely that moment, they heard Ula shush the crowd from the steps of the school.

"You'll have to excuse me," Marc said, finding regret in his voice. "I think that's my cue to head toward the action."

"Before you run off," Andrea said hastily, "we want to borrow you tomorrow, if you don't mind? Can you spare an hour?"

Clearly, Andrea was up to something, and there was no time for details. "Yes," Marc said, watching Hallie for a few more seconds before disappearing into the crowd.

From her position at the front of the crowd, Ula addressed the gathering. "We thank you all for coming," she said with a strength of voice that defied her years. "However, we seem to be missing our esteemed guest of honor. I personally phoned the governor's mansion to invite Tritewater"—hisses and jeers from the crowd—"to our little soiree in his honor this afternoon. But it appears he had more pressing concerns." To wild cheers Ula mimicked someone imbibing alcohol from a bottle.

She was feisty. Marc would give her that. That was the great thing about being truly old: you no longer squirmed at what people might think of you. You just did want you felt needed to be done. And, at least in Ula's case, had a bit of zesty fun doing it.

"Perhaps our good friends of the media will relay a short

message to His Gubernatorial Munificence," she continued snarkily. "Hyrum Tidewater, tear down this hall . . . of learning over my dead body!"

The crowd roared.

"There were a few things Traitor Tidewater"—snickers from the audience—"forgot to tell you when he graced us with his presence on this very spot the other day. He told you that he wanted to bus our kids to the Meagher County School District. But he forgot to mention that the average grade-point per pupil in Meagher District is significantly lower than the average grade point at our 'inefficient' Tippy Canoe Academy. He wants to bus our children an hour each way to dumb them down!"

Applause, boos, and hissing.

"That's Big Brother at its finest, I tell you what. Heil Hyrum! Heil Hyrum! Heil Hyrum!"

With gusto, the townsfolk took up the chant. The media, Marc saw, could scarcely believe their good fortune. Sleepy Tippy Canoe would lead the Montana newscasts tonight for sure.

"Before we take a moment to light a fire under our beloved governor," Ula said, gesturing to the huge papier-mâché head of Tidewater that she intended to set afire as the grand finale, "let me say one more thing about our so-called elected representative. He might not care to honor the sacrifice—and vision—of the pioneers that built this academy, brick by brick, some one-hundred and seventy years ago. But we do. He might not honor his own heritage. But we will.

"You see, friends, Governor Hyrum Tidewater might slur us by mocking the name of our so-called 'Tipsy' Canoe, but I'm afraid we aren't the ones tipping the bottle!" Again she mimicked someone drinking alcohol. Again the crowd showed their enthusiasm.

"If he were paying any heed at all, Hyrum Tidewater would know that not only did his own great-grandfather, Konrad Orenthal Tidewater, both attend and graduate from Tippy Canoe Academy after growing up in our great town"—gasps from some of the audience—"but so did his great-grandmother, Eliza Jane Finlayson. In fact, if Hideous Hyrum were paying any heed at all, he'd realize that without this beloved, historic academy, he wouldn't have been born! More's the pity."

Laughter and astonishment from the crowd.

"As I said, he won't honor his heritage. But we will. My fellow citizens, I hereby declare a new, honorary name for our venerable school—the Konrad Orenthal Tidewater and Eliza Jane Finlayson Tidewater Memorial Academy of Highest Learning."

Fierce applause and jubilant shouts of support.

"Now, my fellow Tippy Canoe-ers. Lend me your voices as our long-serving, true-blue-to-Tippy-Canoe deputy, Lyle Greathouse, does us the honor of lighting a fire under our governor! Heck no, our school won't go! Heck no, our school won't go!"

A flash of flame engulfed the papier-mâché likeness of the governor as the crowd enthusiastically followed Ula's verbal lead.

And after it was all done, the media made sure to get angry sound bites from every riled-up resident willing to vent on camera.

Bull's-eye, thought Marc.

The next day, Hallie agreed to meet Andrea at her home again. When she pulled up, Andrea and Marc were sitting on Andrea's front porch—in winter. Andrea had her leg propped on a stool. All that was missing was sunbathing clothes and lemonade.

"You two are crazy," Hallie said, walking toward the house. "It's bitter cold out here! And you're lounging around like it's a summer day."

"It's almost forty degrees," Andrea said with a laugh. "That's the warmest it's been in weeks. It probably sounds loony to someone from balmy California, but it feels great to get out of the house for a few minutes and breath some fresh, above-freezing air."

"You'll catch a cold," Hallie said. "I didn't even want to get out of the SUV. Not with its seat warmers."

Marc stood and walked toward her. "Well, let's get you back inside the SUV before all that warm air disappears."

"I've asked our handsome mayor"—Andrea gave Hallie a wink behind Marc's back—"to give you the VIP tour of Barefoot Caverns. I'd go myself, but . . ." She gestured at her cast.

"I'd be proud to introduce you to Tippy Canoe's claim to

fame. It's a perk of the office to take all the pretty newcomers on the tour." Marc held out his arm to escort her back to the car. "How about it?"

"I accept." Hallie blushed up to her eyebrows. She felt like a teenager, thinking, *He said I was pretty!* And then, her natural caution surfaced. *Remember, Hallie,* she said to herself, *you're leaving town forever just as soon as the business is sold. He's not a puppy, and you can't take him home with you.*

On the other hand, she thought, *there's no harm in getting a private tour from the town's most eligible bachelor. No harm at all.*

Yep. That was her story. And she was sticking to it.

Inside the cave, Hallie was having a good time. Which was a little bit of a surprise. She had pictured cave slime, bats, and dirt. The only caves she had seen were the ones on Saturday night horror movies. But this place was exquisite, and the artist in her couldn't help but notice every small detail.

The crystal clear, shallow ponds of the Lake Room were enchanting. It was the kind of place you could imagine faeries coming for a drink or even diving from the glassy rimstone dams for a pleasant, languid dip in the water. The Gothic limestone columns, the draperies, and the flowstone (or the "earthworks," as Marc called them) were each fragile art and a beautiful mystery— like a snowflake.

"It's hard to imagine now, but roughly one hundred and fifty years ago, this cave was discovered accidentally by prospectors," Marc was saying.

They were walking through a narrow passageway of rock, moving from the Lake Room to the Hanging Garden. If Hallie looked carefully and caught the light just right as she walked, the rock walls glittered. The effect was beautiful and otherworldly.

"The prospectors were hoping to find gold or silver or anything that could be taken out of the ground for cash," Marc continued.

"The way the story goes, it was a hot summer day. One of Tippy Canoe's earliest settlers, Peter St. Joer, was riding his horse through the hills here when he passed through what felt like a small column of cool air. He jumped down from his horse to investigate, and when he landed, one of his boots sank into the earth up to his ankle. When he tried to pull it out, the ground started collapsing. St. Joer thought that, at any moment, he and his horse might find themselves in a sinkhole of some kind. So he unlaced his boot, left his sock, and rode home with one foot booted and the other barefoot."

"That's a great story," Hallie said. "And I don't believe a word of it."

Coming to a halt in the dim passageway, Marc turned to face her. He was grinning widely. "Well, you should, because it's true. The actual remaining boot he rode home with is on display in the little cave-history museum. The St. Joer family donated it to the town about twenty years ago. You'll see it at the end of the tour."

"Seriously, you're not teasing the dumb tourist?"

"Cross my heart. Besides, you know a better way to find a cave?"

Hallie snickered. "A map," she quipped.

"Smart aleck." Marc's eyes twinkled with humor and then lingered on hers. The pair was surrounded by the soft light and reflective gleam from the rock walls around them. When Marc turned to continue through the passage, Hallie found she was actually disappointed. There was, after all, something inherently romantic about being in such close proximity to a tall, dark, handsome stranger, surrounded by the almost candle-like electric lights that were artfully tucked around the cave.

"What did he do? Send out a search party for his boot the next day?" Hallie asked. It wasn't that she was fascinated with the story, though the history was interesting in its own way. If she were being honest, she mostly liked the sound of Marc's voice. Just like the finest chocolate, it was rich and thick—and she wanted to hear more of it.

"Actually, a sandstorm came in that night." Marc faced her again. "Blew dust everywhere. St. Joer went back several times to find the boot he'd left in the earth, but he couldn't ever find it again. About a year later, another prospector by the name of Kimball Nielson happened upon the boot, still sticking out of the ground. Nielson had heard of St. Joer's adventures—the Blue Moon Silver Mine had been discovered by then. Nielson broke through and explored into the cave a little ways, as far as he dared go with only the supplies he had on hand. He thought there might be agate stone that could be quarried from the cave, and he tried to file a prospecting claim—only to discover Peter St. Joer had already filed a claim over the whole area and had named the claim Barefoot. And the name stuck. As names go, today it sounds a little smaltzy, like a gimmick that someone made up. But it's actually historic."

"The name grows on you," Hallie said. "It has a certain abandon and childlike wonder to it."

"Well put. I like that. I'm going to steal that and use it." The light from the nearest alcove made Marc's eyes sparkle. Or maybe they were like that naturally.

Butterflies made themselves at home in Hallie's stomach. She felt like a teenager with a schoolgirl crush, hoping to impress the boy she liked. It had been longer than she cared to admit since she'd last felt this way—not since the early days of her relationship with Finn. She felt alive.

At the remembrance of Finn, the butterflies turned to lead and sank in her gut.

"So what do you think?" Marc said after they finished their tour.

"The cave was a lot more than I'd expected," Hallie said honestly. "I guess I've always sort of thought of caves as dank places infested with bats and blind scorpions."

"Oh those," Marc said deadpan. "I thought I brushed that scorpion out of your hair before you'd noticed it."

But Hallie was wise to him. "Nice try." *He's definitely flirting with me*, she thought. She had no idea what to do. Part of her wanted to return the energy he was giving off—it felt good to have this kind of energy in her life again. But another, more sensible part remembered why she was here and how soon she was leaving.

It would probably be wise to put the brakes on this thing before she *really* started to like him.

She decided to shift to a more businesslike persona in an effort to put distance between them. "As a tourist attraction, this cave has financial potential—even in Montana's winter season. I believe it could be the white knight your local economy needs, Mayor Greathouse."

"Yeah? What do you see?"

Business-Snob Hallie thought for a minute but came up blank, so Artist Hallie let loose to share her perspective.

"The biggest surprise to me was the darkness," she found herself saying. "Rather than being frightening, there was something poetic about the darkness framing every nook and cranny, the literal thickness of the absence of light, if that makes any sense. It was womb-like, I guess. And such patience! The quiet dignity the mineral world shows in its determination to compose something of beauty, unconcerned whether we, with our human eyes, ever view it or not. It's extraordinary."

Silence.

Hallie worriedly chewed her lip. She had probably come off too hoity-toity or like a rambling lunatic.

Marc said nothing, just looked into her eyes. Then he reached out and squeezed her hand. "I think you said it beautifully."

17

Armed with pork rinds and cold pizza—he'd heard the Deans loved both—Flash borrowed a snowmobile from a buddy and set out for Dimple Hollow.

Approaching the yurt, the noise of the snow machine gave him away as he'd planned. The twins came running out to see who was approaching, but Flash played it cool, pulling right up to the front of the yurt.

"You know what's what, you big donut!" one of the twins said in a singsong voice, glancing repeatedly at him. He noted that both men twitched nervously.

"Move your mutt, Scuttlebutt," the other replied, also in a singsong cadence.

"Betel nut, army hut, onion cut by Old King Tut."

Unsure what to make of all this, he decided to plunge ahead.

"I was over at the Plum's Pantry, and your mother, Barb, told me I might find you here." Flash put on a trusting face, hoping to lull the twins into his web. "I've come to see about hiring you for a job I need done, and I brought you these." He handed over the junk food.

The Deans lit into the cold pizza ravenously.

"I've got myself a problem. I'm on a bit of a deadline, and there's just too much for me to do alone," Flash lied. "I bought this piece of land that the government wants cleared right away."

The twins continued wolfing the food as if they didn't hear a word.

"I need someone to take a chain saw and help me out. And it all has to be done tonight."

"C-c-can we k-ee-ep the chain saws?" asked one of the Deans.

This was going to be easier than he imagined.

The day after touring the cave, Marc's thoughts were still tussled up, keeping him from focusing on any of the hundreds of other things he needed to take care of.

He felt a connection to Hallie, without a doubt. Yet part of him—maybe even a large part—wondered whether he should allow himself these feelings.

Before the cancer, he had thought he would spend the rest of his life with Kathlyn, his wife of twelve years. Just less than three years had passed since he'd faced the terrible burden of burying his wife, the love of his life. He wondered what she would think if she could see him now, grappling with these feelings.

And if he were being honest with himself, he had another concern. If ever he allowed himself to fall in love again, what if he lost another lover to death? He knew the mere thought was morbid, but the way Kathlyn's life had unexpectedly been cut short . . . He just wasn't sure he was ready to open himself up again to that kind of pain and loss, no matter how remote the chance. The fear of facing loss again was real.

"Listen to this," Ula Blackboro said, bringing him back to the present. In her hand was a letter containing a bank draft for one hundred dollars. "I graduated from Tippy Canoe," read Ula aloud from the letter that accompanied the money. "This isn't much, but please accept it to use however you see fit to help save the academy."

Since the television and newspaper coverage of Marc's altercation with the governor, letters had begun arriving at city hall, many of them sent by alumni of the Tippy Canoe Academy. And many of the letters included a donation.

"Love the way you stood up to Tidewater," Marc read out loud after opening another envelope. He held up a fifty-dollar bill that had come with the note. "This is to honor the vision of the Tippy Canoe pioneers in my family lineage. Long live the academy!"

Marc scanned the piles of mail blanketing his city hall desk. "There must be a couple thousand dollars here."

"I never even thought to ask for donations," Ula said. "What if we did? We could have some kind of fund-raising campaign and ask the alumni to help us."

"I don't know that we could come up with a hundred thousand dollars."

"We could ask for corporate donations—or even sponsors. Surely there are alumni out there who have started successful businesses or made something of themselves in the corporate world. We could offer something. You give the academy five thousand dollars, we'll name a classroom after you."

"Couldn't hurt to try." Marc shrugged. "Call the state first, though. Make sure this is legal and on the up-and-up."

After meeting with Ula, Marc finally closed the mayor's office so he could handle his other pressing business. The Greathouse Family Christmas Tree Farm was now just one day away from opening for the season, albeit a shortened one.

Just this afternoon, Marc had finally been able to hire four young men to work as tree-cutters. Two of them had worked previous seasons and could train the others. His father would be posted in the warming tent to take money and hand out hot chocolate and donuts to customers. Marc himself would hand out the eight-foot-minimum height-measuring sticks and answer the inevitable slew of questions about which trees were which, why someone might pick a blue spruce over a Ponderosa pine or Scotch pine, and how much a twelve-foot tree cost.

It would be a busy three weeks, but it wasn't the daunting workload that had Marc worried. In a good season, the farm could sell six hundred Christmas trees. With trees selling anywhere from fifty dollars for the minimum eight-footers to one hundred or more dollars for the really tall, twenty-year-old pines, the farm stood to make roughly thirty-five thousand dollars.

Everything depended on this being a good season. He had to have that cash to hand over to the taxmen when they realized that the promised check was not coming. Hopefully, if he could prove it was forthcoming, he could save the tree farm from the tax lien sale. But with the farm opening more than a full week after Thanksgiving, a full quarter of the four-week sales season had been lost.

On the bright side, he'd only have to pay his employees for three weeks of work instead of four. That would mean some savings. And judging from the number of calls that had come in from residents wondering when they could gather their family for the annual tradition of choosing a live, local tree, there was demand for the trees.

Marc just hoped there was at least thirty-five-thousands-dollars' worth of demand out there. If he didn't make the money in the next three weeks . . . well, he didn't want to even think about that.

It was time to go to the farm and make it work.

19

The day after touring the cave with Marc, Hallie called Andrea and agreed to drive her over to the lunch meeting for the Tippy Canoe Business Association. She still felt a little guilty that she was the reason Andrea couldn't drive herself. Plus, Andrea made a definite point: if Hallie planned on getting locals to take over Christiansen's, the meeting was the best place to find them.

"So?" Andrea said as Hallie drove.

"So?"

"I'm dying for details of your cave tour. Accompanied by our fine-looking mayor."

"I had a great time. The cave was lovely," Hallie said, being purposely coy.

"And?" Once again, Andrea had a mischievous gleam in her eye that Hallie was quickly becoming familiar with.

"You're incorrigible, aren't you? And nothing. He's a good-looking man, and a great conversationalist. But the timing stinks. I think that he's still struggling with the loss of his wife. What did you tell me her name was?"

"Kathlyn."

"Right. Kathlyn. He's still dealing with that. And I'm just here for a few more days. And frankly . . ." She paused. "The prospect of having to deal with my own dead husband is a little daunting. But I can see what you're trying to do. You and my Aunt Edna could start a matchmaking business together. You'd probably make a fortune."

Instead of laughing like Hallie expected, Andrea was silent for a moment. "You're a quick one," she said finally, her voice quiet. "I hope you aren't offended. And I know I've only known you for a few days now. It's just that . . . well, Marc needs to see the possibilities, if that makes any sense. And I've sensed the same thing about you, if you don't mind my being so bold as to say so."

Hallie felt a real bond with Andrea and appreciated the well-meaning effort. There was something about almost killing someone that brings people closer together. Andrea may not have known Hallie for very long, but her perception was dead on. "I hadn't really thought about it before, but you're right. I could probably use a bit of a push toward the deep end of the pool, so to speak. I've never been the kind of person to open up to men easily, especially after what happened between me and Finn. I really did have a good time touring the cave yesterday. And I won't lie. Marc is an attractive man. Very much so. It felt good to have someone look at me like that again."

It occurred to her that Andrea was really in much the same boat as Hallie and Marc when it came to dealing with the loss of a spouse. "How about you? Have you tried putting yourself out there to meet someone?"

"Touché," said Andrea with a small laugh. "You've got me. It's always easier to push your friends into the pool than to jump in yourself."

"If someone came along?"

"Okay, okay. I cry uncle. I won't send you out on any more cave tours with handsome mayors."

"Hey, I didn't say that." Hallie laughed in mock protest. "No, seriously, Andrea. If someone came along, and you felt a spark of kismet, could you seize the day?"

"*Carpe diem*," Andrea quipped. "I'm going to say yes, but only on the condition that you won't put me to the test."

Both women laughed.

At the meeting, Hallie was welcomed warmly. Everyone came up to shake her hand and introduce themselves—about three dozen business owners in all, including all of the tenants of Christiansen's as well as attorney-slash-restaurateur Bob Greathouse of Plum's Pantry. Browsing the catered buffet, Hallie decided this was the kind of social gathering she could get used to. Cucumber-turkey-cranberry sandwiches on ciabatta bread, creamy havarti, baby Swiss slices on multi-grain crackers, and braised fresh pineapple, not to mention the sophisticated sweets provided by Hers: Chocolate.

Clearly, her stereotyped expectations of these people had been far and away off base. She hadn't exactly expected those who lived here to be bucktoothed, banjo-playing, chaw-chewing inbreds, but she hadn't expected Italian-artisan-bread finger sandwiches and Danish cheese, either.

So maybe Montana wasn't half bad. After all, she still hadn't been accosted by a moose.

After some good-natured munching, gossiping, and milling about the room, Hallie heard Andrea bringing the meeting to order.

"Ahem, excuse me, everyone. Welcome!" Andrea turned to Hallie. "We're kind of informal here, but I did want to make sure everyone had a chance to meet Hallie Stone, who's taking over Christiansen's. Hallie, you might not know this, but Finn was actually the chairman of our little group. Let's take a moment, in silence, to recognize Finn's influence on our community, and the hole his absence leaves in our midst."

The group observed a reverent silence.

"Thank you," Andrea said after an appropriate length. "Seeing as how Finn was gracious enough to be our fearless leader, I think it only natural that his replacement—"

Oh no. Realizing what was about to happen, Hallie felt gooseflesh erupt over her arms and neck.

"—be the same woman who is taking over his busi—"

"No," Hallie said to the room, hoping she had quelled the panic in her voice. "No, no, no." She forced a smile.

"No time like the present to dive into the deep end of the pool," quipped Andrea with a Cheshire-Cat grin.

Hallie thought fast. Turnabout was fair play and all that. "While you honor—and frighten—me with the suggestion," she said, summoning a mischievous grin she hoped mirrored Andrea's good-natured countenance, "I know you're really just trying to pay me back for ruthlessly running you down on Main Street and breaking your leg."

To Hallie's relief, the group broke out in laughter. "Deferring to her much greater knowledge and experience in this arena, I humbly nominate Andrea. She'd make an excellent fearless leader—especially with the pain medication the doctors have got her on."

The laughter was even louder and longer this time. *Whew,* thought Hallie.

"I accept," Andrea said after the din had died down. And without missing a beat she added, "But only if you'll be my cochair. By acclamation, then. All in favor?"

A chorus of applause echoed throughout the room, mixed with chuckles.

"Sneaky," Hallie said to Andrea with a wink.

"Well played. You're a quick wit."

Hallie felt the exploration of the deep end was unearthing a whole new aspect of her personality. She kind of liked it.

For the next hour, the group discussed the need to dramatically increase the number of visitors to the cave—especially over the holiday and winter season, when tourist numbers were at their lowest. Money was the fly in the ointment. There was no budget for an advertising campaign, no matter how small, let alone anything grand.

Worse still, with all that had gone on in the past few days—the mayor slugging the governor, then Ula mercilessly roasting Tidewater all but literally—the township was getting terrible press at the least. At the worst, it was quickly becoming the laughingstock of Montana.

What to do? No one seemed to have an answer.

"You know," Hallie offered, unsure of where this suddenly upward-bubbling knowledge was coming from, "in philosophy and battle strategy, there is a principle called strategic reversal."

"A feint," one of the group said. "You make your opponent think you are moving in one direction. Then, at just the right moment, you reverse and take another route. A classic strategy."

"Oooooh, a battle strategy." Andrea's eyes shone with excitement. "I feel so Sun Tzu and *The Art of War.*"

"Well, I don't know about that." Hallie feigned a grimace. "I was just thinking that if the media are so anxious to capture every crazy antic of Mayor Greathouse and Ula . . ." She realized she couldn't remember the woman's last name.

"Blackboro," someone interjected.

"Ula Blackboro—thank you—then maybe we should turn the tables. Maybe we could use the media, instead of them using us"—she paused, realizing she was including herself, even though she'd been here less than a week—"using us as their hapless target. If we play our cards right, we could get an ad campaign for free."

Hallie didn't know why she was putting her two cents into the town pot, but it felt good. Oh dear, it was nearly official: she'd gone native.

There were murmurs of approval and piqued interest.

"Fantastic," Melora said, wearing rose-colored quartz earrings today—still the size of small boulders. "How does it work?"

"I just come up with the ideas." Hallie held her hands in front of her. "Someone else has to do the heavy lifting."

"We need to draw the attention of the media," Melora's husband, David, said.

"An event," Bob Greathouse said, continuing the momentum.

"A winter festival," offered someone else.

"A Christmas cave festival," chimed Andrea. "A big to-do. Something worth making the trip from Bozeman for. Or Billings."

The room was energized. Something was happening. Everyone, including Hallie, was getting caught up in the fervor. The town was going to battle—for its own economic survival.

At that moment, a great noise shattered the air.

Marc Greathouse slammed through the doors of the building, his face purple with rage.

"The tree farm," he said, suddenly looking faint, "has been destroyed."

20

Exhausted after a bitter, cold night keeping an eye on the Deans, Flash slept the day away. Luckily, the storm threatening snow had held off, and the twins had been as good as their word, working without a single rhyme of complaint. In exchange, he'd given them some cash—a hundred bucks each—and the chain saws.

Flash chuckled to himself. They'd actually seemed to have fun shaving the sides off each tree.

Not anxious to get out of bed, he thought about ordering in some food. Best to lie low and not be seen around town. There was no way anyone could link him to the twins. He'd worn a fleece snowmobile mask and sunglasses when he'd visited the yurt. Supervising their chain saw work that night, he'd worn the snowmobile mask again. And anyway, Flash was sure they hadn't been able to see him too well in the moonlight. Naïve as they were, the brothers had never even thought to ask his name. That had disappointed him because he'd spent time planning the fake name he'd give them—Grinchley McScrooge. They were so dumb that he was sure they wouldn't even have gotten the joke. Now he'd never know for sure.

Still, it was done. Now the deal could go through, and he would show all the people in this stupid town. All the people that scorned him. Didn't give him the respect he deserved.

After ordering for delivery, Flash reached for the television remote. All he had to do for the rest of the day was relax. Tomorrow, after it was clear word had spread around town of the vandalism at the tree farm, he could probably even call a real estate agent and make Marc Greathouse a lowball offer on the land.

He turned on the television. But as the picture filled the screen, Flash didn't believe his eyes. A "Breaking News" banner was blinking on the screen, and Mayor Marc Greathouse was being interviewed.

Worst of all, he was standing in the middle of the destroyed tree farm.

A well-dressed woman shared the screen with images from the previous day's set of press conferences.

"There have been rumors swirling today that some of Governor Tidewater's supporters might have even ordered the attack on Mayor Greathouse's Christmas tree farm in retaliation," the reporter gushed. "We have just learned, minutes ago, that a spokesman for Governor Tidewater has denounced the Christmas tree vandalism and promised that there will be an investigation. The governor himself is apparently unreachable for comment."

No, no, no, no, no. Flash couldn't believe what he'd just heard. *This can't be happening.* His whole plan was spinning wildly out of control. *It was supposed to be quiet and under the radar.*

The reporter was turning to the mayor now.

"You have made some enemies in the past few days," she said. "Do you have any idea who might target you like this?"

Marc shook his head. "No idea. Politics is one thing, but this . . ." His voice trailed as he gestured to the ruined Christmas trees surrounding him. He looked like he might start to weep on live television.

"Will you replant the trees?" the reporter asked.

"Christmas trees take at least twelve years to grow," Marc said, looking physically ill. "This farm is finished. We'll have to let it go. After being laid off at the Blue Moon Mine, this was my only real income. I'm ruined."

"Just devastating," the reporter said, turning to the camera. "A terrible crime has been committed, leaving this town's mayor with a bleak future. You can count on this news team to bring you the latest on Governor Tidewater's investigation into who committed this Christmas crime."

The newscast moved on to other topics, and Flash pressed the mute button.

He hadn't counted on this level of attention. The Deans came into town regularly. They were sure to get wind of the controversy and come forward with a confession. They would at least tell their mother, and she'd go straight to the authorities. She'd probably demand a full investigation to find out who duped her sons into doing this.

Flash needed to lie low and start looking for an exit plan.

allie met Bob Greathouse for lunch at his restaurant, Plum's Pantry, to discuss her legal options. They had little time before the next business alliance meeting.

"You can sell Christiansen's, you can hire someone to manage it, you can close it down, or you can run it yourself," Bob said, stating the obvious. "The real question is, what do you want to do?"

If you had asked her four days ago—even two days ago—the answer would have been, hands down, to get rid of it and put it all behind her.

Now, she wasn't so sure.

There were pros and cons to each option. Half the residents of Tippy Canoe had left within the past year, he reminded her. They had left behind a glut of foreclosed homes and not a few empty storefronts. Selling Christiansen's would mean taking cents on the dollar of what the place could be worth in a better economy. And that was only if a buyer could be found—a big *if* when you factored in the hay rent and the Seuss twins in the basement.

Money wasn't really the biggest motivating factor here. She

was making more than enough through the sales of her artwork. She just wasn't sure what to actually do with the place.

Closing it down would benefit neither Tippy Canoe's Main Street business district nor Hallie. Running it herself would mean leaving her life and studio in California—not an option. She had grown fond of the little town, but not that fond.

Bob was confident it wouldn't be hard to find someone to manage the storefront rentals, collect the rent, and keep up on the maintenance. But that was only if Hallie could convince the tenants to pay rent in actual money rather than in hay and milkshakes.

The whole thing was horribly depressing.

On the upside, the lunch is great, thought Hallie, trying to find even the thinnest silver lining. She couldn't help but notice that Bob was only picking at his own food. She asked him if there was anything wrong.

"Just my own business woes," Bob said, attempting a weak smile. When Hallie gave him a confused look, he continued. "All the food we use here at Plum's is grown on the same land as the Christmas tree farm."

Hallie gasped. "Was it damaged with the vandalism as well?"

Bob stood to clear their plates. "No. But then it didn't have to be. Betty and I didn't find out until yesterday, but the land is behind on its taxes. Without the funds from the trees, the lien won't be paid in time, and the land will go to auction next week. With our greenhouses on it. I'm afraid that this will probably be my last winter garden. There's no point in Plum's staying in business without it." Bob tried to keep a brave face, but the smile on it was shaking.

As Bob walked away, the door chimed, telling Hallie that the other business owners were arriving for the emergency meeting of the business alliance. Sadly, Plum's wasn't the only business in town in danger of closing.

This was the battle plan: the business alliance would put on a Christmas Cave Festival. Everyone was pitching in to make the arrangements.

"We will offer special candlelight tours of the cave through Christmas Eve," Andrea announced to the business owners who had gathered once again, this time to finalize the details of the town's Christmas promotion. "We'll use those battery-operated, flameless candles so there won't be any damage to the cave. The academy choir students have agreed to perform in the cave's Grand Ballroom, the main cavern where locals once held dances many years ago. As a special touch, flameless candle luminaries will line the walkways in the cavern.

"Also, I spoke with each of the churches, and as a way to help us all remember why we actually celebrate Christmas, they've agreed to host a live Nativity inside the Grand Ballroom. And the carolers will sing as part of a short narration of the Christmas story," Bob said.

Betty walked over to her husband and drew an arm around his waist. "Also, the city council has decided to hold the annual town Christmas party in the ballroom after the very last tour."

That drew excitement from everyone in the room. Apparently the Christmas party was a highlight of the year for a lot of folks.

After settling the group down again, Andrea went on about how each of the tours would be run over the next few weeks.

"And I'm excited to tell you that at the end of each cave tour, an old Tippy Canoe tradition will be revived," Andrea said gleefully. "When I was a girl—do any of you remember this?—we used to tour the cave each winter as a school class. Do you recall how we ended the tour?"

For a moment there was a perplexed silence.

"I'll give you a hint . . . to ward off the winter chill outside, before walking back to the school, we had—"

"Hot snow-chocolate!" Brooklyn Teasdale said, wearing a "Hers: Chocolate" apron over her impossibly large pregnant belly.

"I had forgotten all about that. At the end of the tour, hot chocolate magically appeared in one of those big, five-gallon thermoses, and—"

"And then the teachers would tell us to go and find clean snow to put in it so we didn't burn ourselves," Melora Post added, a new, even larger, pair of geodes hanging from her ears. "Yes! I'd totally forgotten about all that. That was so fun."

"That was back in the days before political correctness," David chimed in. "If a school teacher did that today, there'd be a lawsuit."

"Maybe we should reconsider," Hallie said with hesitation. She couldn't imagine picking up snow from the ground and plunking it into her hot chocolate. There were limits to her newfound adventurism.

A voice hollered from somewhere in the back, "Just remember to stay away from the yellow snow."

The room broke out in a wide array of guffaws and giggles.

"No, no, we should do it." Brooklyn was getting excited, beaming from more than just the expectant mother glow. "I mean, we're not going to force anyone. We'll just make the suggestion. And it wouldn't cost much at all to offer shaved ice, you know, for anyone who's less adventurous. Or from California." She winked at Hallie with a wide grin.

They agreed that a special "Tippy Canoe Christmas Elf Shoppe" could be set up in the visitor's center, and each of the local stores would get space inside to sell unique Christmas gifts.

"Everyone needs to chip in," Andrea said. "And then a percentage of the money raised could go toward improvements in the cave. The cave's got a maintenance list a mile long."

As a sort of Christmas present, every visitor to the cave would be given an assortment of coupons and special offers from local businesses. These would serve as an enticement for tourists to shop and eat before they left town.

"The academy students have even volunteered to line our Main Street business district with luminaries too." Andrea held one of them up to show the group. "We'd just need to come up with the money for white paper bags and votives. I thought maybe each business could sponsor the luminaries needed for the front of their store. That way, each of us would only be paying a few dollars."

Considering the economic tailspin the town was in—and how pinched each of the business owners was feeling as a result—it was a top priority to make sure the whole Christmas Cave Festival could be carried out fast and cheap.

"There's only one thing left to discuss," Andrea declared. "How do we get our free ad campaign, so that anyone knows we've got this great festival going on?"

It was time for Hallie to throw on that newfound, outgoing personality and take center stage.

"Okay, I must have drawn the short straw 'cuz this was my assignment. And as you can see, I have brought in a special guest to be with us today. She doesn't own a business. But I think we'd all agree, after what's happened in this town in the past few days, that she might know a thing or two about how to manipulate—I mean befriend—the media." Her aside was rewarded with several chuckles and guffaws. "So, everyone, please welcome Ula Blackboro."

Ula beamed as a smattering of clapping echoed the room.

"So, Ula," Hallie said. "Our little alliance needs to get all the free publicity we can for our last-minute Christmas Cave Festival. Got any media-savvy ideas for us?"

"Easy," Ula answered flatly. "Just send them a special invitation."

The business owners laughed, until they slowly began to realize that Ula wasn't making a joke.

"We just send them an invitation, and they'll come?" Melora asked incredulously. "That's it? Will that really work?"

"Well, as I see it, you've got two things going for you." Ula settled in to break it down for everyone. "First of all, the weeks before and after Christmas are really the slowest news days of the year. So television and newspaper reporters are desperate for any interesting story."

"How do you know that?" Hallie asked. Then, realizing her question might have sounded a bit harsh, she added, "I mean, you sound like you know from experience."

"Sort of," Ula admitted. "My grandson is a television reporter in Spokane. I called him to get his take on it."

A chorus of impressed "aahs" and "oohs" rippled over the room. It did make sense, the whole bit about Christmas being sort of a news dead zone. After Black Friday, nothing really exciting happened event-wise until Christmas Eve. Unless you lived in LA, where high-speed chases were a regular news filler. The pieces started to fall into place in Hallie's head.

"I think I see where you are going, Ula. Human interest. No one can resist a cave," someone in the back said.

"And the media love to be coddled," Ula continued. "So you send them a special invitation, telling them that there will be a media-only cave tour on such-and-such a day, at such-and-such a time, and that they will be allowed to film and take photographs, and that there will be caroling children in the cave, and luminaries, and it's the first time this has ever happened, and that you'll have local officials here and lined up for easy interviews. You'll have them eating out of your hand."

Ula paused, actually blushing slightly. "At least that's what my grandson said."

"I say we go for it."

"Can't hurt!"

"Won't know unless we try."

"Then it's decided," Andrea concluded. "Everyone, let's get to work. Let's save Christmas in Tippy Canoe."

Hallie was happy. She was fitting in and feeling more comfortable with the small-town atmosphere. No longer the outsider, she felt included.

As people began to filter out to the parking lot, out of the corner of her eye, Hallie saw Melora make a quick gesture to Andrea.

"Where's Barb?" Melora asked. "She never misses one of these meetings. Is she feeling okay?"

"Um, she's fine," Andrea answered. But the hesitance in her voice alerted Hallie, who was trying to listen without seeming to eavesdrop, that something was not right.

Marc had wracked his brain endlessly for the past day, trying to think of someone he could have pissed off enough to ruin the farm. Was he the intended victim? Or the Greathouse family in general? His dad occasionally had to break up a fight or hold one of the local drunks until they'd slept off the effects of the alcohol.

As for himself, Marc never really minced words, and that had made him a few enemies over the years. As mayor, sometimes he had the unpleasant task of denying someone a permit. Maybe this was a referendum on his mayoral term. Maybe Dickie Hatch was still pissed at being tromped in last year's election. He was working in an advisory job with the governor's office now.

Then there was Tidewater himself. Could this be his promised retribution? The man had little sense of ethics and even fewer brain cells, but surely he was smarter than to pull off a stunt like this.

Wasn't he?

The thought that Marc's actions might have directly or indirectly lost the farm made him physically ill. But truthfully, he'd felt that way ever since telling Grandpa Bob and Grandma Betty about the upcoming auction. Losing the farm was bad enough, but the possibility of losing Plum's was unconscionable.

Without anything to do at the ruined Christmas tree farm but wallow in misery and what-ifs, Marc went to see if he could be of any use in the mayor's office—focusing on the academy's money troubles rather than his own.

Another day brought another couple dozen letters from alumni and others wanting to express support for keeping the academy open. And once again, many of the letters contained donations. Marc counted out nearly fifteen hundred dollars, bringing the grand total to just over thirty-five hundred.

Great, Marc thought to himself snarkily. *Just another ninety-six thousand, five hundred to go. We can come up with that. No problemo.*

From the hallway outside his office, Marc heard Ula calling his name.

"In here," Marc called, as if there were many other choices. There were only two other tiny rooms in the city hall-half of the trailer.

"I'm afraid I'm the bearer of bad tidings," Ula said glumly. "We're in bigger trouble than we knew."

Marc looked up, feeling even more deflated . . . if that were possible. "What's the news? Just hit me with it."

"Remember how our beloved Governor Tidewater stood on the steps of the academy and said we'd need at least a hundred thousand dollars to keep this school open?"

"How could I forget?"

"Well, it turns out he really meant a quarter-million dollars."

"A quarter million!" Marc couldn't keep the shock out of his voice.

"I called the state to make sure my whole fund-raising campaign wasn't off base, and when we started discussing numbers, I was informed that the hundred thousand dollars is what is needed just to keep the school open with a bare-minimum staff. There would be no school lunch, no bus drivers, no janitors, no teacher's aides." She paused for dramatic effect, leaning toward him. "That's not the worst of it. There would be no extracurricular programs. No sports, no cheerleading, no field trips. And here's the doozy. No marching band."

Marc couldn't believe what he was hearing. Without the marching band, the academy just wouldn't be the academy. The school was known far and wide for its requirement that every student play a band instrument every year. The academy was not only the only school in Montana to ever win a national marching band championship title; it was also the only school in Montana to ever be invited to nationals. And the academy had been invited not once, not twice, but thirteen out of the past twenty years. The community held bake sales and raffles to raise the money needed for the band to travel to nationals wherever they were held. Never once had the school had to turn down a nationals invitation because of lack of travel funds. The so-called Band Parents group met regularly, and hundreds jammed into the academy every spring for the band's big, year-end community concert. Simply put, the Academy was a marching band school. Closing down the music program was unthinkable.

Almost as unthinkable as trying to come up with a quarter-million dollars by January first.

"What do we do?" Marc said quietly, not speaking to Ula so much as he was speaking to himself.

"Did we get any more donations today?"

"Fifteen hundred dollars."

Ula just looked at the floor.

"This is a fine kettle of fish," Marc said, throwing his pen. "It's moments like this when being the mayor is no fun. I don't want to have to tell our fellow Tippy Canoe-ers that we can't afford our own historic pioneer academy."

"We have to do something," Ula said quietly. "There must be a way."

Marc gave a half-hearted laugh. "This certainly hasn't been a bright and cheery Christmas season so far. I've already been on CNN News twice: once, for punching the governor and being arrested by my own father.; the second while nearly crying over the wreckage of the tree farm. And now I'll go down in Tippy Canoe history as the mayor that closed down the academy. At least things couldn't get much worse."

There was a knock at the door.

"Come in," Marc called wearily.

An unfamiliar man walked into the mayor's cramped city hall office. "I've been trying to catch you for days."

"Sorry, who are you?" Marc said.

"Tim Brotherton, *Bozeman Daily Chronicle*."

Marc began to remember the man now. This guy had been at both press conferences—one of the faces in the media horde. "What can I do for you?"

"I'd like to request an interview."

"I'm a little snowed under right now, as you can see." Marc gestured to the drift of mail covering the desk.

"Looks like a lot of cash," the reporter observed, unperturbed.

"Donations," Ula said curtly, scowling slightly at the man. "Tippy Canoe Academy alumni have begun sending in donations to help save the school, ever since—" She stopped.

"Ever since the media started to tell your story?" the reporter offered, barely keeping the irony from his voice.

"Maybe you could catch me tomorrow." Marc looked the man in the eye, willing him to go away.

"I've been trying to catch you ever since I got into town." Tim did a quick tally on his fingers. "Four days ago. What are the office hours here, anyway?"

"I'm the staff," Marc repeated his favorite line. "I'm the mayor; I'm the mayor's assistant; I'm the janitor, the secretary, the town punching bag." He resisted adding "media punching bag" to that list. After all, this guy was right. All this money sitting on the desk was here because the media had told Tippy Canoe's story.

"Office hours are whatever day I can get here, starting when I arrive, ending when I leave. It's a small town. Everyone pitches in, and everyone does what they can."

"This is important," Tim said. "Urgent, even."

Marc looked at him coolly, not saying a word.

"And you're the top elected official in Tippy Canoe. So I'm requesting an interview."

"In a nutshell," Marc said diffidently, "what's this about?"

"We've had some calls," Tim said deliberately. "Calls saying there might be irregularities with the city accounts."

Ula gasped.

"Specifically, Mayor Greathouse, concerns that you might be involved with irregularities." Just to drive the point home, Tim drew a slow gaze over the cash on the mayor's desk.

Tippy Canoe's oldest, feistiest resident turned ash white. Marc was afraid she'd fainted in her chair.

"Where there's smoke, there's fire," Ula Blackboro said, the color having returned to her cheeks. "But in this case, I just hope the old saying isn't true." She looked gravely at Marc. "I've known you since you were born. I grew up playing with your mother, God rest her soul. If you tell me that none of this is true, I'll believe you."

She waited, expectantly.

Sitting across the desk, the *Bozeman Daily Chronicle* reporter was also waiting, a no-nonsense expression welded on his face.

In that moment, Marc remembered a quote that had hung on the wall next to the dinner table in his grandparents' humble home. It was from Charles Dickens's timeless novel, *Great Expectations*. It was a quote spoken from Joe to Pip: "Lies is lies. However they come, they didn't ought to come, and they come from the father of lies, and work round to the same. Don't you tell no more of 'em."

Marc knew that if he lied now, he would have to keep lying. And the lies would only grow bigger.

The jig was up.

Tippy Canoe was in the news again, as Flash lay low for a second day, . But this time, he was happy to see that the upset over the ruined Christmas trees got only minor coverage, with reporters mentioning briefly that no culprit or motive had been identified.

The television journalists spent much more time on a lighter note—the news that Tippy Canoe would host a Christmas Cave Festival.

"Joining me now are Andrea Linford, who runs a fourth-generation business in Tippy Canoe, and Hallie Stone, who has come all the way from Malibu, California, to become the town's newest business owner. Together, they are heading up the Christmas Cave Festival."

"Great," Flash spoke back to the television. "Just what we need: more Californians coming to take over Montana."

The last one, Finn, had come trying to take over everything, thinking he was all special because he came from the big city. *Who did Finn think he was, making eyes at Flash's wife? Good thing the SOB was dead, or I might've had to kill him*, Flash thought.

He grew increasingly irritated as he listened to the two women enthusiastically discuss the hot snow-chocolate, the live nativity, and all the other holiday crap they had planned.

"Some scholars believe that the humble manger Jesus Christ was born in was actually a cave used to feed and shelter livestock from the weather. Hosting a live Nativity inside the cave will be a very special way for families to pause to remember what the season is really all about."

"Like you really care what the season is about," he scoffed at the obnoxious, preachy woman.

The California lady said all cave visitors would receive a special Christmas gift of coupons and special offers.

"Some gift," he snorted. "That's the real reason for the season. You're just out to make a buck."

"Some people may ask if Tippy Canoe has put this festival together because recently political events have cast your town in a bad light and hurt tourism," the reporter said. "How would you respond?"

"It's the elephant in the room, and as business leaders we are not going to shy away from it," the local lady said, looking directly into the camera. "Controversy has cast a spotlight on our town recently. I think I speak for everyone when I say that we are not comfortable being the center of this kind of attention. But there is another story here to tell."

"The economy of Tippy Canoe took a hard blow when the Blue Moon Mine shut down," the California bigwig interrupted. "Those businesses that have survived are hurting. The town is fortunate to have a literal hidden gem, courtesy of Mother Nature. Barefoot Cavern tours will help your family create Christmas memories you'll never forget, especially with all our special events."

Throwing his glass against the wall, Flash yelled, "What do you know about the Blue Moon Mine!" He was really angry now. "You waltz into town, looking to get rich by marching tourists through our cave. But no one wants to do anything to help the little guys who sweated taking silver out of the Blue Moon, only to be thanked with three months of severance!" He couldn't stand fat-cat business owners looking to make a quick buck, especially outsiders—like the California broad.

The interview was over, and the newscast moved on to a cooking segment. But Flash was lost in thought.

His problem was simple. Sooner or later, the Deans were bound to say something to their mother about being hired to use chain saws on the Christmas tree farm. With all the media attention, law enforcement would be under pressure to follow any lead.

Somebody else might find out about the real value of the farm, then Flash would be toast.

He needed to make a preemptive strike—something to send everyone on a wild goose chase. He needed to divert the heat just long enough that Marc Greathouse would accept an offer to sell the farm.

And then Flash could collect his riches and get out of slow-poke Montana forever.

He could go to Hawaii and find some pretty little woman to entertain him. There were plenty of women out there willing to show some affection to a man with lots of cash to blow. Or he could go to Cancun. He'd seen something on television once about wealthy Americans who move permanently to the beaches of Mexico to enjoy the high life at rock-bottom prices. And those dark-haired Latina women . . .

All he had to do was concoct a story wild enough to get the whole town buzzing down the wrong track. A story so impossibly bizarre that everyone would believe it. Or want to believe it, anyway.

I've got nothing but time on my hands, he thought. *And I always have fancied myself a bit of a storyteller.*

"And maybe while I'm at it, I can teach that California fat-cat a thing or two," he said out loud. "Yeah, that's exactly what I'm going to do."

Sitting down at his computer, Flash began to type.

Hallie was sitting inside Kobold Trading Company, just having watched herself on TV, when there was a knock on the shop door. Through the glass she could see Andrea Linford, crutches under her arms, waving.

"I saw your rental car and thought I'd stop for a moment," Andrea said cheerily as Hallie opened the door to let her in. "Megan dropped me off at the Ledger-Register a while ago so I could try to catch up on some work at the office. I was just hobbling over to Plum's for a bite of lunch."

"You have no idea how happy I am to see a friendly face. This is the first time I've been back in here since, well—"

"Since the night you and the Deans scared the daylights out of each other," Andrea finished. "You're brave, coming back here alone."

It was easy to feel brave with her friend here . . . and a baseball bat next to the door. Hallie had learned to expect the unexpected in this little town. A moose might very well pop out of the bathroom.

"Have a seat." Hallie brought out a chair from behind the sales counter. "Would you like another chair? To prop your leg up on?"

"Would you mind? I have to admit it is throbbing. Trying to crutch my way over to Plum's probably wasn't my brightest idea. But my stomach was yelling louder than my leg was!" She gestured to the crutches.

"I'm starving too," Hallie said, helping Andrea situate her cast. "I could go for another one of those Scottish egg salads with a Boysenberry popover on the side. What if we called in an order? Then I could run over and pick it up for us."

"You don't have to ask me twice."

"I figured I'd have to face this place again sometime," Hallie said between bites of the warm, buttery popover smeared with jelly. "But only in broad daylight. At least for now."

Andrea asked whether Hallie was planning to open the store for business.

"I don't think there's any way I could run a store." Hallie laughed and wiped a dribble of juice off her chin. "The cash register would probably revolt. I'm much more comfortable with my brush and paints than with buttons and thinga-ma-jigs." She gestured over to the counter with its computer, register, and some other unknown gizmo. "Thankfully, being an artist doesn't require a whole lot of technology. "

"The creative type. I should have guessed!" Andrea exclaimed. "What kind of art do you do?"

"Oils, mostly, though I do some sketching and watercolors. But professionally, I'm an oil painter."

Andrea wanted to know all the details, and Hallie found herself explaining her work and her journey to becoming a working artist, which led to explaining how she and Finn met and fell in love, spending romantic days and nights painting together. Until Hallie's success had torn them apart.

"Finn never whispered a word about painting during the whole time I knew him," Andrea said, taken aback. "How strange that he would give up painting totally after leaving you in California. He must have had it bad for you."

Not bad enough, apparently. He still left.

"Oh, I'd be really surprised if Finn gave up painting." Hallie sighed thoughtfully. "It was in his blood. A part of him. But there's a dark side of being an artist—the critics, the buyers, the constant worry that your work is terrible and no one will like it. I think that's the part that he gave up." At least she hoped.

Because it would have truly been a shame if Phineaus Kobold had let the pressure extinguish his creative spark. She understood what fear could do to a person. To let the world stand in judgment of your work—that was the worst, most frightening part of daring to believe you could be an artist. Hallie remembered in the early days it had taken all her willpower to traipse from gallery to gallery in Los Angeles, hoping just one might recognize talent in her art. Most of them had turned her down flat. She'd almost given up. Finn had been the one that kept her out there, kept her going back. Finn had believed in her first, even before she'd believed in herself. Without the courage he'd lent her, she never would have walked into the one gallery where one of the dealers believed in her vision and finally said yes.

But when it was her turn to support him through the lean times, he was too proud to accept. Or too stubborn. Or both. Hallie hoped he hadn't been so pigheaded to stop painting all together.

"There's one way to find out," Andrea said..

"Find out what?" Hallie asked, coming back into the conversation after the musings in her head.

"Whether Finn was painting. He had the whole top floor of this building. It must be huge. The way you talk, I'll bet he's turned a corner of it into a studio. Maybe there's art all over the place up there." Her eyes glittered with intrigue.

"I don't know." She had thought about it, of course. The space would have to be looked at sometime. But she wasn't ready to face Finn's stuff—to be among his things, in his house, knowing he would never be there again. Or worse, to discover that no trace remained of the man she had once loved.

"Someone's got to clean out the refrigerator," Andrea said, putting a hand on Hallie's leg. "You know, check up on things up there." She looked up at the ceiling.

Hallie knew it was true. She just didn't want to be the one to do it.

"I'm going up." Andrea lifted her cast off the chair where it had been resting, and, using her crutches, lifted herself to standing position.

"You're kidding me!" Hallie said, laughing. "Andrea! You'll never make it! You'll hurt yourself. You'll fall down the stairs. You'll break your other leg! The town would never forgive me!"

Both women enjoyed a good laugh.

"I'm tougher than I look," Andrea said in mock seriousness. "A lesser woman might have killed herself by skidding her motor scooter under your enormous, rented Yukon. But no, no! Not Andrea Linford! I put up a fight that Yukon won't soon forget!"

Hallie was giggling uncontrollably by this time. Andrea gave over to the giggles too.

"Seriously," Hallie said, catching her breath. "Sit down and finish your salad. You can't do those stairs with that cast."

"Seriously," Andrea said, not missing a beat. "Of the two of us, who's the cripple here? You don't dare go downstairs. You don't dare go upstairs. You don't dare operate the cash register!"

Put that way, Andrea's logic did offer Hallie a new perspective of herself. She'd only meant it as a joke, but it struck a chord deep in Hallie's gut.

Either that or she had indigestion.

"Up or down," Andrea said with mock defiance. "I'll do one with you. I don't think my leg will do both. Which is it—the Deans in the basement or the demons upstairs?"

25

Upstairs or downstairs—neither option seemed terribly appealing.

"You don't think the Seuss twins are in the basement now?" Hallie hoped for a reassuring answer.

"Seuss Twins?" Andrea asked, her left eyebrow drawn up in to a high inquisitive arc. Her lip quivered.

Hallie clapped a hand over her mouth. "Oh my gosh! Did I say that out loud? Was that horribly insensitive? It's just what came into my scattered brain when I met them. They were wearing red long johns, had wild hair, and rattled off incoherent rhymes. They looked like Thing 1 and Thing 2 from *The Cat in the Hat*. So ever since, I've been calling them the Seuss twins in my head."

Now she'd done it. Andrea looked like she was turning purple. Hallie had probably mortally offended her new best friend.

Andrea finally let out the breath she had been holding in a giant belly laugh that reverberated throughout the store. "That's actually pretty perfect for them. They're harmless, and they mean well, but they do tend to get into mischief from time to time. But they shouldn't be here. Barb and the elder Greathouse put up a yurt for them to stay outside. They must not have wanted to face the Wicked Witch of the West again," Andrea said, slapping her knee, then wincing at the unintended pain it caused.

"Okay then, basement it is." Hallie might very well be the Wicked Witch of the West, because she was still scared enough to make Andrea go with her, bum leg and all.

Traversing the narrow stairs to the basement took some time, with Hallie going first and helping Andrea down, step by step. Andrea's boot made a *clunck clunck* sound as it went down each step. But they made it to the blue-glass knobbed door without mishap.

Going through the door, the basement seemed smaller to Hallie than it had that night. And this time, light from the windows gave the space a decidedly less sinister atmosphere.

"Hello!" Andrea called out. "Anyone down here?"

"Hello?" Hallie echoed, bracing herself just in case.

"Lyman? Lehman? Are you down here?"

A pleasant silence was all that met their ears. No wiffling.

"Let's go all the way back, just in case," Andrea said. "You won't have really tackled this fear if we just stay by the door."

It was clear that no one else was in the basement. No people anyway. "So Andrea," Hallie started nonchalantly, "you don't suppose there is any way there could be some furry animal or something hiding down here."

"What, you mean like mice?"

"No. Close though. I was thinking more like a moose," said Hallie, going for an offhand tone of voice.

"A moose?" Andrea asked incredulously. "Why on earth would there be a moose in the basement?"

"Oh, no reason."

Andrea didn't seem to buy that answer for a second. "I can tell there is way more to this than what you're saying. Must be some weird, city folk thing."

"Must be." Hallie was not about to launch into the backstory for her horrible moose phobia. Her friend would probably die from laughter.

Slowly, the two women made their way to the darkroom in the back corner, talking as they went about the arts-and-craft décor, the dilapidated state of the basement in general, and the possibilities for turning the space into something useful. Or at least cleaning it up. Hallie could tell that her friend was keeping up a steady conversation in part just to keep Hallie focused on something other than her anxiety. Andrea's thoughtful kindness made Hallie grateful. She might never have come down here again if left to fend for herself. And it was a beautiful space with real potential.

At the end of the great room, the darkroom door was open, as it had been that night.

"Hello? We're coming in," Andrea said one last time, the tone of her voice making it clear to Hallie that Andrea was saying the words just for effect—not because anyone was there to hear them.

And she was right. The darkroom was empty. A switch outside the door lit the small room. The sleeping bags were still there on the floor, and there was half a bag of pork rinds and fast-food sandwich wrappers in a trash can.

"No ghosts . . . or moose," Andrea said with a wry smile. "Just some trash that needs to be taken upstairs."

Hallie took the trash can and followed Andrea back toward the former sitting-room area. Andrea sat down on one of the boxes, and Hallie perused the old books in the lead-glass cabinets jutting from the walls. The mahogany glowed in the sunlight, and opening the cabinets brought out a rich, musky odor of antique wood. Hallie breathed in deeply, luxuriating in the fragrance. And then sneezed after breathing in all the dust too.

"We've got to do something about Barb," Andrea said randomly.

Hallie shrugged. "She doesn't like me. Something about me running over her best friend." Hallie had meant it as a joke, but neither woman laughed. In that moment, Hallie remembered the enigmatic conversation she'd overheard between Melora and Andrea after the business alliance luncheon. Barb hadn't been at the second alliance meeting, either.

"Barb's been avoiding me," Hallie said, certain of the truth. "She's been avoiding the business alliance meetings because I've been there."

Andrea looked up, the surprise obvious on her face. "You are very perceptive." And then, "I've been wanting to mention it to you, but I wasn't sure what to say. It isn't your fault, really. Barb and I have been friends since, well, since before Washington crossed the Delaware. And she's always been a bit sensitive. That's who she is." Andrea paused. "It was just the way Barb found out about the accident from you, you know . . . I think it startled her. I think she felt like you were a little unrepentant, like maybe you didn't care—not that I think she's right about that. As I've gotten to know you, I don't think that's what happened. I'm inclined to think you were maybe a bit traumatized yourself. In shock, you know."

For the second time that afternoon, Hallie found herself grateful that she'd finally let her guard down and allowed herself to return the unlikely friendship of Andrea. "I didn't mean to offend Barb. I was upset and my brain was still in California. I admit that I came here with the wrong attitude . . . I think I was afraid to walk into Finn's new home and have everyone think I was a gold-digging, not-quite-ex wife. So I was determined to put everything about it in my rearview as soon as possible. I'm sorry I was so standoffish to start."

"I understand, and I'm glad that I've had the opportunity to get to know you with your defenses down," Andrea replied. "Barb is one of my best friends in the world, and I'd love to see you two come together. I know we could all be great friends. That is, if Tippy Canoe will be seeing more of Hallie Stone in the future."

That was the big question, wasn't it?

"I have a suggestion," Andrea said.

"I'm all ears," Hallie said. The two women had made their way back up the stairs to the Kobold Trading Company. The remains of their salads had wilted slightly in their absence.

"You're an artist. You know how it feels to have someone appreciate your work. You and Barb are on common ground there. Barb's been painting for years. She's even taught a couple of classes for the on-again, off-again Tippy Canoe Arts League."

"Really? What does she paint?"

"Lately she's been doing paintings of Tippy Canoe's historic homes. A few years ago, one of the earliest pioneer homes in the valley burned to the ground. Ula Blackboro—you met her at the last meeting—wanted to put a written history and photograph of the house in the Sons and Daughters of Montana Pioneers archive. When no one could come up with a photo, Barb painted the house from memory."

"What a wonderful idea," Hallie said, meaning it sincerely. "I might be biased, but I think a painting of a historic house would be even better than a photograph. It's more—" She searched for the right word and gave an exasperated shriek when her inner thesaurus failed her. "Ugh! I can't think of it. You know, more of a tribute to its story than just a random Polaroid." She gasped falsely. "Or worse, a digital photo."

"That's it exactly!" Andrea chuckled. "Now if only Barb had been here to hear you say that, this whole thing would be water under the bridge. I'm positive of it." And then, she added, "Since that first painting, she's done a few more. You should see the one she did of the old founder's building. That's the arts-and-crafts style house farther down Main Street. Barb has that painting and a couple more framed and for sale over there at Plum's, but no one pays them much mind."

"So your suggestion is a sort of art-for-peace, hippie-dippy, coming together of the right-brained minds," Hallie said with a laugh and held up a peace sign. "Right on, man. I accept."

26

"I loaned myself some money from the city sewer improvement fund," Marc Greathouse said slowly, unable to meet the eye of Ula or the journalist. "Dad had just told me that he was about to lose the Christmas tree farm to a county tax auction because he apparently owes all these back taxes and—"

"How much?" the journalist interrupted.

Marc took a breath. "I didn't steal it. That never was the plan. I was going to pay it back. With interest. I was going to use the money from selling the Christmas trees."

"How much?" Ula spoke softly.

At that moment, Tim Brotherton's cell phone began to ring. He ignored the call and continued to glare at Marc.

Meeting his eyes, Marc answered. "Thirty-five thousand dollars."

"Thirty-five thousand . . ." A distressed noise escaped from Ula's lips.

Tim's phone rang again. This time he glanced at the display screen, a confused look creasing his forehead.

"The Christmas trees have been destroyed," Ula said sadly.

"You have no way to return the money back to the city now."

"I didn't go through with it." Marc hung his head low. "I did take the money from the sewer fund and deposit it in my personal account. I even wrote the check from my account and mailed it to the county assessor. But then I"—he decided it best to skim over the details here—"I asked for my letter back at the post office, and I shredded it. And I took the money back out of my personal account and put it back into the town sewer fund account. I know the whole thing was rash and poorly thought out. And I'm sorry. I regret that I ever moved the money in the first place. But nothing came of it. I can prove it. I didn't spend the money."

Tim's phone went off again. A third call in as many minutes.

"Excuse me one quick second," Tim said, speaking to Marc and Ula.

He could take all year as far as Marc was concerned. What really baffled Marc was how this reporter had found out about all this anyway. Had Marc forgotten to clean up some detail as he'd moved to return the money? Had he still committed a crime, even though he'd given all the money back?

Tim stood just outside the door and answered the call on his cell phone. "I'm in an interview."

A pause while the reporter waited for a response on the other end.

"The mayor of Tippy Canoe."

Another pause.

"Now?"

Tim looked at Marc, who was squirming in his seat. It was extremely awkward and uncomfortable to know the reporter was talking about Marc while he was still in the room.

"I don't think that's a good idea," Tim said into the phone.

The reporter turned toward the wall, his back to Ula and Marc. "What's it say?"

During another long pause, Marc was ready to crawl under a rock somewhere. Or at least under the desk.

"Hold on for one second," Tim said into his phone. He turned to face Marc again. "You have a fax machine in this office?"

As Marc told Tim the fax number, Tim repeated it into the cell phone.

Seconds later, a fax began to print.

Taking the fax from the machine, Tim handed the paper to Marc. "I'd like you to take a look at this, please."

Marc took the fax.

An open letter to all residents of Tippy Canoe:

It is time for the secrets in this town to stop! We have all been humiliated by the bizarre behavior of our mayor and his cronies. Now is the time for the truth to come out!

The mayor destroyed his own Christmas tree farm. Why would he do this? He is hoping to fool everyone, but don't be taken in! To save his father's precious farm from the tax lien auction, he became desperate. He was let go from the Blue Moon Mine, and he could not get a loan. Running out of time, he made a deal under the table with Tippy Canoe's newest wealthy business owner. Her name is Hallie Stone, and she owns Christiansen's. She has come to our sleepy, unsuspecting Main Street business district to run her drug cartel while pretending to have a sudden desire to own a business in our dying town.

For many years, the mayor has been hiding his secret use of marijuana. Through his drug connections, he found out about Hallie Stone's operation. He threatened to expose her unless she agreed to help him. He blackmailed her, forcing her to loan him the money he needed to save the farm. Then he forced her to hire the innocent Deans to ruin the Christmas trees on his father's farm. The trees were worth more dead than alive, and he is plotting to use the insurance money from the destroyed trees to live off of because he has no job. And Hallie Stone gets to keep her undercover drug cartel.

For my own safety, I cannot reveal my identity or tell you how I came to know this dark secret. My life would be in danger if I was found out. I know this story is unbelievable. But if you don't believe what I have exposed here, there is an easy way to check to find out whether this is true. The Deans were given some cash and two chain saws in payment for their work. The mayor's father even helped the Dean twins build themselves a yurt in exchange for their work. Yes, this scandal reaches so deep that even the mayor's father, Tippy Canoe's only Sheriff's deputy, is in on the crime. If you ask them, they will tell you the whole story.

Maybe now the residents of this town can understand the mayor's recent, bizarre outbursts. The mayor and Hallie Stone must be stopped! Please take action to save our town and protect our children from drugs and corrupt politicians! It is time to take a stand for Tippy Canoe!!!

None of this is true," Marc stammered, utterly floored. "It's all lies."

Ula took the fax from his hand and began to read.

"I have no idea whether Dad has insurance on the tree farm. I don't even know if you can get insurance on a tree farm. I'd be happy to take a drug test to prove I don't smoke marijuana or take any other drugs, for that matter."

Ula continued to read.

"Have you or your father had any business dealings with these people the letter mentions? The Dean twins?" asked the reporter.

"None," Marc said definitively.

"Did your father help them set up a yurt? That is very specific information if it's a lie."

"Of course not," Marc snapped. "I don't even know what a yurt is."

"Do you have speakerphone on your telephone here?"

"I think so."

"Let's call your father."

His heart pounding, Marc dialed his father's number. As the

phone rang, he placed the call on speaker. His father answered.

"Dad, it's me. Marc."

"Hello, son."

"Dad, I have a strange question for you. Have you ever heard of something called a yurt?"

"Sure. I just helped the Deans set one up over on the ridge above Dimple Hollow."

Marc's gut fell to the floor, and bile rose to the back of his throat. He coughed it away.

"Dad," he spoke into the speakerphone. "Something's going on. I'm going to have to call you right back."

"That's fine," Lyle responded, his voice sounding perplexed. "I'll wait right here until I hear back from you."

Marc told the reporter and Ula that he was going to call the Deans' mother, Barb, over at Plum's Pantry. He dialed the number, leaving the phone on speaker, Tim and Ula listening as it rang.

"Plum's Pantry. Barb speaking."

"Barb, it's Mayor Greathouse."

"Marc, how are you?"

"Barb, have you seen this open letter that I guess is circulating?"

"Open letter?"

"Do you have a fax machine over there at the café? I'd like to fax you over something to read right away if you can."

Barb gave him the number. Tim faxed a copy of the letter to the café.

"I'd like to stay on the line with you while you read it, if you don't mind," Marc said to Barb. "You should probably know that I've got Ula here with me, and a reporter from the *Bozeman Chronicle*."

"Is anything wrong?" Barb's voice belied concern.

"Yes," Marc answered, without elaborating.

"Here's the fax coming through. Okay, I'm reading it now."

Marc, Ula, and the journalist waited.

From the other end of the line, they heard Barb gasp. And

then, after a pause, Barb said, "I knew I didn't like that Stone woman. Knew it from the moment I met her."

"Keep reading, Barb," Marc said. "The letter mentions the Deans."

Barb fell silent. And then, for a second time, she gasped. After another silence, they heard her gasp a third time.

"Okay, I've finished the letter." Barb's voice was completely emotionless and flat.

"Have you spoken to your sons lately?" Marc asked.

"Not in a couple days," Barb said slowly. "Not since your dad took me out to spend a night in the yurt with them." And then she lowered her voice. "Speak of the devil. I'll give you one guess who just walked in. Our good friend from California."

"We'll be right over."

28

Hallie and Andrea had agreed it would be best if Hallie went to Plum's alone. That way, Barb wouldn't feel like Andrea was forcing Hallie into something. After taking Andrea home and seeing her inside, Hallie decided to strike while the art-for-peace iron was hot. She walked over to Plum's.

One corner of the café was devoted to displays of tourist trinkets and other things for sale. On that fateful night when Barb had kicked Hallie out, refusing to finish her order of eggs and toast, Hallie had seen the stuff but hadn't paid it any attention. The next day, she had been too frenzied when she ran away from the Dean boys to notice anything.

Now, though, she saw there were three framed paintings on the wall. They were not displayed in very good light, Hallie noted. And while the frames were custom matted, they were cheap. Both were classic mistakes of an amateur artist, the marks of someone who lacked confidence in their work.

But the paintings themselves were truly excellent. Hallie studied them. Each featured a historic house, rendered in careful detail, but in a way that gave the homes a soul. They weren't landscapes; they were portraits. The art brought Hallie back to art school when she'd studied two still-life paintings by the eighteenth-century French painter Jean-Siméon Chardin at the Getty Center in Los Angeles. Chardin could take a few pieces of fruit on a table and speak something of what it is to be alive, to be captured forever in your prime. That's what Barb had done to these homes—she had elevated them, capturing a moment in time that would never exist again. They were an homage to the quiet dignity of those who'd spent their lives in humble Tippy Canoe, each generation adding to and influencing the next.

Hallie loved them, especially the painting of the founder's building. She relished the opportunity to see what the home must have looked like before time had put a hand of age and wear to it. A handwritten note on each identified the name of the home and a price. The prices were laughably low—Barb was asking thirty dollars for each. It was clear from the details that she had spent hours upon hours on each. For that effort at these prices, it was less than minimum wage. Hallie had to buy all three, and not just to get on Barb's good side. She genuinely liked them. Carefully, she started to take one of the paintings off the wall.

"Don't. Touch. Those." The voice that spoke the words was harsh, unyielding. Turning around, Hallie confirmed her fear— Barb had spoken the words. Hallie was startled to see Mayor Greathouse, Ula Blackboro, and a young man Hallie didn't recognize standing next to Barb. All four wore serious expressions on their faces.

Hallie felt like she had been caught red-handed. But doing what? She hadn't run over anyone lately. She hadn't frightened any more locals.

"I love—" Hallie started.

"I said don't touch them," Barb cut her off. "We've had just about enough of you in this town."

There were a few patrons in Plum's, but the place took on that eerie silence where one can hear every intake of breath. Hallie had purposefully decided to look at the artwork first to try and see a different side to the grumpy old woman. And she had; these paintings showed light and joy as well as a talent to see the good in things.

But now Hallie was at a loss because Barb could clearly not see any good in her. The vehemence in Barb's voice—it was as if the woman thought Hallie was a common criminal.

"I wanted to buy them," Hallie said meekly. "I thought they were for sale. I wasn't trying to take them without your permission."

She fought hard to keep her voice from cracking at the end. Hallie had done nothing wrong, yet she felt like she had been judged and found wanting. The amount of ill will being directed her way was crushing.

"We know who you are," Barb growled. "And why you've come to our town. And how you're trying to spread your evil to my sons."

What is she talking about? Hallie felt like someone had thrown her into deep water without enough warning to fill her lungs with air.

"Hold on," Marc said, gently touching Barb on the shoulder—his stony face softening. "We haven't heard her side of the story yet."

"We haven't heard your side of the story yet either," snapped Barb, glaring at Marc. "If I find out it's true that you're in cahoots with this woman"—she glared at Hallie now—"and you've done something against my twins . . ." Her snarled voice trailed.

Hallie felt dizzy with confusion. She had a nearly overwhelming urge to shove her head between her knees.

Ula held a piece of paper out to Hallie. "What is the meaning of this?"

Hallie took the sheet of paper, her confusion mounting. It appeared to be an email sent to the *Bozeman Daily Chronicle*. "I've never seen this before."

"Read it," Ula and Marc said in unison.

Hallie started reading aloud, her voice faltering and then falling silent as she continued down the page. As she finished, she stopped breathing altogether. The world shrank into darkness with only the smallest pinprick of light.

Without warning, her knees buckled. She reached to steady herself, and found herself sliding slowly down the cold wall to the floor.

She was going to be sick.

"None of it's true," she said. "None of it."

29

To Marc, it was obvious the woman was telling the truth—he recognized in her response the swooning sensation of having taken a mental blow. He himself had felt the same way reading the letter only minutes ago.

He was surprised to find himself feeling relief. He hadn't wanted to believe this woman could be involved.

What he could not understand, however, was why this was happening. A growing dread welling in him indicated that they would find the letter's part dealing with the Deans to be true. If that were the case, someone had gone to great lengths to implicate four innocent people in a well-woven tangle of lies.

Try as he might, Marc came up blank attempting to think of a single person who might have the motive to ruin four lives.

To Barb, he said, "Why don't you go round your boys up, and we'll call Lieutenant Oster over. Don't worry. We aren't accusing them of anything. We can get to the bottom of this without scaring the twins. With any luck this whole letter is someone's idea of a sick joke."

Barb didn't look happy, but it was clear to everyone that there really wasn't any choice in the matter. Marc needed to get Oster over to question the boys, and his dad was waiting for a return phone call. Better to kill two birds with one stone.

Walking to the corner and pulling out his phone, Marc dialed up his father. "Dad, it's me again. We have a bit of a situation over here."

Marc gave him the rundown without too many of the details, temporarily leaving out any mention of the almost-borrowed city funds. "So we need Damon down here to get a statement from the Deans. Since you're implicated in this letter too, it's probably best if you didn't ask any of the questions."

"Good thinking, son. This just makes me sick. That Stone women seemed so nice too. Do you think she had a hand in any of this?" Lyle Greathouse asked between crackles on the phone.

"I think it's about as likely as me having ruined those trees myself," Marc said in Hallie's defense.

"Well, that's good then. I'm really starting to like that woman," his dad replied.

"Me too, Dad. Me too," Marc said and closed his phone.

30

Time lost all meaning to Hallie. She was sitting on the ground, the cold linoleum floor chilling her bottom. But it was still no match for the chill that had settled in her gut. At some point, Bob and Betty Greathouse must have arrived and ushered Hallie over to the quiet corner booth, because that's where she was sitting. Though for the life of her, she couldn't remember getting there.

"It's all right, dear," Betty said with a little pat. "Everything will work out just fine. You'll see. After this, you should come over and tour our winter garden. You haven't had a chance to see it yet. And with the auction, there might not be another chance. It'll help take your mind off of all this. You'll see."

In a daze, Hallie's head nodded of its own accord.

Bob walked back over to the table after conferring with Lieutenant Oster, Deputy Greathouse, and Marc. "The Deans just got here, and Lieutenant Oster is talking to them real gentle. Don't worry. Everyone knows you had nothing to do with this," he said reassuringly.

Not everyone. Hallie looked over at Marc talking to his father by the front door. Then there was Barb, just a few booths away, standing over her two boys like a mother hen. Lieutenant Oster was in the middle of getting a statement from the Deans. Barb was still shooting Hallie dirty looks with enough heat to burn down Main Street.

This sleepy, little town had struck again, pulling the rug out from under her when she least expected it. And just when she started adjusting to the small-town life too. Homesick for her own bed and view of the ocean, Hallie wondered if she should just drive home to Malibu right then. Let the moose deal with Finn's estate for all she cared. It just wasn't worth it.

Andrea flashed to mind. And then all the other new friends and memories she had made: the Teasdales; crazy beehive and buffaloberry Judy; Melora, Melora's earrings, and her husband; the Greathouses and their amazing food; Marc and the cave; the Christmas festival. There were so many good things she had discovered in this town. She wasn't about to let some anonymous jerk with an email account take it from her.

"Do you think it would be okay if I listened in—from a distance, that is?" Hallie inquired of Bob.

"If that's what you feel is best, I don't see why not. After all, this does concern you, and you have a right to know what the Deans have to say. I'll go over with you," Bob offered.

"I appreciate that," Hallie said, scooting out of the booth and walking over to the interview in progress.

"So it's true that you boys wrecked the Christmas trees?" Lieutenant Oster followed up carefully to a previous question.

The Dean on the left looked much the same as the night in the basement, except he had swapped out the long johns for a green flannel shirt and camo vest. He started nodding when the other brother—Lehman?—noticed Hallie there for the first time. "The what from the donut, shut mutt in the gutt, strut, strut!" he exclaimed, pointing to Hallie.

Barb's face turned bright purple with rage when she followed the line of her son's point back to Hallie. "I knew it! I knew you had something to do with this. I will personally—"

Lieutenant Oster jumped in front of the old woman in her mid-launch for Hallie's throat. "Now wait right there, Barb. Let me handle this, please." He directed his attention back to the two men. "Did that woman," he was pointing to Hallie, "ask you to ruin trees?"

The Dean wearing the camo shook his head. "Silly strut, down a jut, and a deli cut, fat mutt, fat mutt."

The other Dean nodded as if the sentence had made complete sense to him. After a moment, he clarified for the rest of them. "She . . . scared . . . sc-sc-screamed at us. So we . . . go a . . . away. We have a y-yu-yurt now. That . . . that's . . . when man . . . c-came. He g-gave us a job."

His twin grinned broadly. "And chain . . . chain saws."

Everyone agreed it would be best if the Greathouses took Hallie on that promised garden tour, since her presence still seemed to agitate the Dean brothers. Lieutenant Oster would continue to try and get a straight answer and a description of the man who had hired them.

Hallie wasn't really sure she was in the mood to go traipsing through a garden. On the other hand, she had nothing better to do. So she agreed. On her way out the door, she thought she saw Marc giving her a small smile and encouraging nod. Barb still scowled, but it was less fierce.

Bob Greathouse said, "I told you it would work out. We'll let them sort it all; it has nothing to do with you now. Everything will be right as rain."

She sure hoped so. But there was still a nagging feeling in her gut that she had not seen the last of this play out yet. After all, someone disliked her enough to implicate her in that email. But who?

And why?

It made her brain hurt to try and plot out the motivations of a clearly villainous man. Maybe a winter garden tour was just the thing to take her mind off things for a while.

Hallie opted to take her own rental car and follow Bob and Betty to the Christmas tree farm where the greenhouses were built. It was a little ways out of town, where the forest became thick and beautiful. Then without warning, Hallie saw rows and rows of scalped trees.

Her reaction was instant and visceral. Who could do this? Be so evil? And why had they dragged her into it?

Betty and Bob led her down a little dirt road, past the trees, to what looked to be a long, plastic roof oddly sitting on the ground. Getting out of her SUV, Hallie was welcomed by the Greathouses and a cold blast of wintery air.

On the east side of the structure, wooden stairs descended into the ground. Betty opened the door, and Hallie gasped, the cold and the shock of the trees forgotten

The greenhouse was warm—California warm. In the eighties warm.

And it was lush. A sea of green plants filled the space. Flowers bloomed in reds, oranges, and purples. The air smelled humid and deliciously earthy. And the entire greenhouse was underground.

Going down a couple more stairs, Hallie took a deep breath. The entire atmosphere was instantly relaxing. "I can't believe this. It's a tropical paradise. I've never seen anything like this."

"This is our geothermal greenhouse," Bob said, his pride obvious in his voice. "No artificial heat, and no electricity. Completely self-sufficient. And we can grow winter vegetables for the restaurant all winter long. We have two other greenhouses just like it."

"I've never heard of a geothermal greenhouse," Hallie said, deciding not to say that she knew almost nothing about greenhouses in general. Clearly, Bob seemed to think the concept of a "geothermal" greenhouse was something special. So if she waited long enough, it would probably be explained to her.

True to Hallie's expectations, Bob explained. "These pipes

underneath the grate you are walking on extend eight feet into the earth." His smiled brightened, and he puffed his chest out slightly. "It's my own invention. I got the idea from my root cellar. Long story short: because my root cellar is always about fifty-eight degrees, all winter long, no matter how cold it is outside, I started to wonder whether I could take the root cellar concept and turn it into a greenhouse. And it's been working great for years. It's what our restaurant has become famous for—fresh, local greens and vegetables all winter, grown right outside our back door."

Betty showed Hallie the gourmet lettuces, explaining the name of each kind, and how they were special winter varieties.

"And all open-pollinated, of course," Betty said. "We don't grow any hybrid seed at all."

Hallie nodded politely, not at all sure what her host was talking about. A lesson for another day, for sure. It occurred to her that this is what other people must feel like when she talked about her art. In her passion for the subject, she often forgot that most people wouldn't understand—or care—about the difference between the English Pastoral school and the French Barbizon school. Clearly, the Greathouses had the same passion about their gardening.

Betty and Bob cooed over the rutabagas, the carrots, the parsnips, the huge shrub-like kale plants, strawberries, and the fresh peas. Hallie knew enough to know that having fresh peas while there was a foot of snow outside was something special. And all without any electricity. It truly was amazing.

The tour continued. There were different kinds of Chinese cabbages and radishes in a dozen colors. There were orange trees and fig trees.

"These zucchini we get by hand-pollinating," Betty said. "But our real pride and joy in here is over here." She led Hallie to the far end of the greenhouse, where she picked up a pot. "Here. Grab a leaf off this and put it in your mouth." She held out a bushy, bright green plant with oval leaves about an inch long.

Hallie plucked one and settled it in her mouth, expecting something minty or lettuce-y. Or, at worst, like dirt.

What she got was a mouth full of sugar.

Betty smiled widely. "Stevia," she said. "It's a plant called stevia. Everyone is making zero-calorie sweetener out of it these days. We use it to make hot chocolate in the winter and lemon balm lemonade in the summer—and our customers love it. It's three hundred times sweeter than processed cane sugar, and just a few leaves go a long way. And over here we have açaí berry and Inca berry. And over here . . ."

"Are our cantaloupes," Bob finished, beaming. "Noir des Carmes. An old, old French variety. They have been grown in hothouses in winter for over four hundred years. We might be the only restaurant in the continental US that serves its own fresh, home-grown cantaloupe all through the winter."

The tour continued for at least another hour. It served the purpose to get her mind off the events of the day. And it served as dinner. By the time she left the greenhouse, she had tasted so many kinds of lettuces and peas and greens that she felt she had eaten an entire salad.

When it was time to go, Bob and Betty showed her out, but opted to stay behind a little longer. The couple was so fiercely proud of all that they had built here, and it infuriated Hallie that, through no fault of their own, it was in jeopardy. That lifetime of love and care could vanish over a dispute with Uncle Sam and someone's villainous intentions.

With the fresh cantaloupe that Bob and Betty had given her for the road, Hallie sped back down the path of ruined trees.

After the winter garden tour, Hallie went to Andrea's home to discuss the latest details of the Christmas tree defrocking. Namely, to vent that she had been accused in a letter of being a drug dealer.

"I mean, this is *me* we're talking about." Hallie stopped pacing for a minute to throw her hands up in the air. "I don't even use ibuprofen, for heaven's sake."

"It's ridiculous. I agree—"

"I know, but that mayor of yours actually believed it."

"Now, Hallie. From what Marc said when he called—"

"He called? Of course he called. That's how the gossip phone tree works in these little towns, doesn't it? I don't suppose he had any ideas on who might want to ruin his life. Not to mention mine and that of the older—and nicer—Greathouses."

"He had a few ideas, but I think—"

"Poor Bob and Betty. They were crushed. Just crushed. I could tell those greenhouses are their whole life. Whoever did this deserves to roast in h—"

"Hallie!" Andrea yelled and stuck out her crutch to halt Hallie in mid rant. "Will you just slow down for five seconds?"

Hallie begrudgingly sat down in the oversized wicker chair opposite Andrea. "I'm sorry. I'm a wreck. First I was catatonic in shock, but now I'm in a worse temper than the art critic who slammed my last piece." Hallie placed her head in her hands. "I can't just sit here. I have to do something."

Andrea placed a reassuring hand on Hallie's knee. "That's what I've been trying to tell you. Marc emailed me a copy of the letter. There was something in it that made no sense."

Hallie gave Andrea a wry look.

"Okay, aside from the whole crazy drug-cartel-conspiracy plot. I think I might have an idea who could have done it."

Andrea reached over to the side table and handed Hallie a copy of the horrid letter. She almost didn't take it. She'd read it once and had no such desire to read it again.

"The writer mentioned a yurt," Andrea pointed out.

Hallie sighed and forced herself to scan through the email once again. "Here it is." She read out loud. "The mayor's father even helped the Dean twins build themselves a yurt in exchange for their work."

"That yurt kit that Barb bought only arrived in town three days ago," Andrea said. "It was only assembled two days ago."

"And?" For the life of her, Hallie could not see where this was going.

"Obviously, whoever wrote this letter not only knew about the yurt, but also knew it had already arrived and been assembled. Barb told me that the only people she'd had a chance to tell about the yurt were Deputy Greathouse and me."

"She could have told someone and forgotten about it," Hallie reasoned. After all, this little town seemed to know when someone had a cold, moments after they sneezed. "The deputy could have told someone. The seller might have told someone. Even the Deans might have donut-strutted their way into telling someone."

"Yes, those are all possible," Andrea said. "But my journalist's sixth sense is telling me that something else is going on. Here's what you don't know." She told Hallie about going to the Plum's Pantry for lunch and asking Megan to run back out to the car to get the two yellow-and-black-striped scarves she'd knitted for the Deans for Christmas.

"The café wasn't very busy, but there was this guy there who was acting . . . hmm . . . strange and dressed even odder. He was covered nearly head to toe with a ski cap and scarves, and he was wearing sunglasses—even inside," Andrea said. "He seemed anxious and nervous. I thought he was eavesdropping on our conversation. He gave me the willies, to tell the truth."

She'd paid particular attention, she explained, because right after she'd asked Megan to go back for the scarves, the man had suddenly gotten up and left.

"Something about him, his manner, his walk . . . it was familiar. Like I knew him. It's bothered me for days. I think I've figured it out, but I can't be sure unless I see him in person again," Andrea said, scooting to the edge of her chair.

Hallie, excited as well, scooted to match. "And this guy: you think he's capable of it?"

"Oh yeah. I'm not sure why he'd want to, but I'm positive that he overheard Barb and me talking about the yurt. So even if we don't know his motive, he had the opportunity."

Hallie jumped to her feet. "Well, let's get going then. I'll drive."

"Hold up there, quickdraw," Andrea said, holding up both hands and chuckling for a moment before getting serious again. "If I'm right—and it's a big *if*—than this man is even more dangerous than I thought. I'm pretty sure we need back-up."

"Who? Marc?"

Andrea shook her head emphatically. "No, he'd probably just as soon kill the guy than let him go through the court system."

"Okay. Well, who then?"

"I have someone in mind. Grab me the phone, please."

Hallie handed the phone over to Andrea and wondered who she might be dialing. David, with a bag of rocks to wield as a weapon? Or Matt, who could tie the bad guy up in fishing line?

"Hello? Tim?" Andrea said into the receiver. "This is Andrea. I have a proposal for you."

33

Apologizing that she couldn't drive because of her broken foot, Andrea asked Tim if he'd mind stopping by her home for a few minutes for a face-to-face chat.

During the exchange, Hallie's imagination was running away with her. Sprinting, even. As soon as her friend hung up the phone, she started in on the interrogation.

"So who's Tim?" Hallie's tone of voice slid up and down, teasing Andrea like a high schooler.

"A friend," Andrea said shortly, not elaborating.

Hands on hips, Hallie gave Andrea *the look*—the one her mother had used whenever she wanted to gussy out the truth.

"Really . . . more like a colleague." Andrea fidgeted with her cast.

"Uh-huh."

Andrea yanked the pillow from under her knee and tossed it at Hallie. Both women broke into schoolgirl giggles.

"I mean it. Tim works for the *Bozeman Chronicle*. In fact, you met him today," Andrea said, once her giggles were under control.

"That young reporter? He was good looking. I approve." A

smile, the first real one all afternoon, spread across Hallie's whole face.

"Don't make me throw my last pillow . . ." Andrea threatened. "Now hurry and help me clean up before he gets here."

Tim knocked on the door five minutes later. Hallie left the drawing room to show him in. But before turning the corner, she just caught a glimpse of Andrea smoothing her hair.

Hallie snorted to herself. Just a friend? Yeah, and a moose was just a really big dog.

When Hallie yanked the door open, she saw the young man from earlier on the doorstep—checking his breath.

Interesting.

Andrea called from the other room. "In here, Tim."

The little smile he had given Hallie widened and brightened, and then he hurried to the next room.

Hallie's own smile doubled in size as well. This was going to be fun.

Andrea and Tim spent a few minutes catching up. Hallie made sure to make herself as small and unobtrusive as possible. She wanted to watch these two interact.

Andrea explained her injury, and for the first time, Hallie didn't feel her hackles rise. Pain and suffering aside, she was glad the accident had happened. She got a new best friend out of the deal. Hallie shot up a quick "thank you" to Dale, Andrea's late husband, just in case he really had arranged the whole thing.

"So what was this you said about a proposal?" Tim said, wiggling his eyebrows suggestively.

"I was hoping you might have time to do a favor for a damsel in distress," Andrea said with a wide grin.

"Absolutely," Tim answered. "You name it."

"In just a minute. First, I want some answers. Lieutenant Oster questioned the Deans. They readily admitted their role in the Christmas tree incident."

"So I heard," Tim said, nodding. "They swear they were hired by a man, not a woman. I interviewed Oster about an hour ago." He paused, deciding to up the ante a little. "But something tells me you already knew that. You didn't call me here just to talk shop."

Andrea lifted an eyebrow. "You're on to me." She paused. "Speaking as one journalist to another, there is one thing that puzzles me about your role in all this."

"My role? I don't have a role. I just report the news, as you know."

"Maybe, maybe not," Andrea said enigmatically, a playful, Cheshire-Cat smile lighting her face. "You showed up unannounced at the mayor's office this afternoon, from what I gather."

"Yes."

"When he tried to give you the brush-off, you told him the interview request was urgent because you'd had calls about the mayor being involved in 'irregularities with the city books.' Those were your words, if Marc and Ula have informed me correctly."

"You've done your homework," Tim said, looking pleased at Andrea's interest.

"After Marc confesses that it's true, you get a call on your cell from your editor telling you about this anonymous email."

"Exactly right, so far."

"So here's my question: How did you know, even before you knew about the email, that the mayor had been helping himself to the town checkbook? Who tipped you off?"

"Would you be offended if I said a good journalist never reveals his sources?" Tim shrugged.

"You've been working for the *Chronicle* for what, five years about?"

"Roughly that. Yes."

"I admit up front that I already know the answer to my next question, but I'll ask it anyway. In those five years, how many times have you come to Tippy Canoe to report a story? Not often enough." Andrea's eyes sparkled mischievously.

Hallie held back a gasp. She was shocked that Andrea was flirting shamelessly with the reporter. Was it a calculated act to enlist the man's help. Or more likely, did Andrea not even realize she was doing it?

"And before today's call about the mayor's 'financial irregularities,' how many calls have you gotten from Tippy Canoe-ers giving you news tips?" Andrea continued.

"Not many, I admit."

"I've run the weekly paper here for a day or two now," she said with a laugh. "I get calls every day from locals with concerns, conspiracy theories, complaints, story ideas, UFO sightings—the whole gamut. I can't go to the grocery store or even to church without being stopped. But on this one, no one called me." She paused. "So I know that no one called you."

Tim's face appeared thoughtful, like he was weighing his answer. "It was a feint. A shot in the dark."

Andrea's eyes glittered, her smug smile saying the she was enjoying her victory. "You made it up."

"I had a hunch something was not right. When I finally got my chance at the mayor, I took it. You would have done the same thing in my shoes."

"Exactly," Andrea said. "That's why I asked you to stop by to see me. I had to make sure you were still the kind of guy who was willing to go out on a limb for a story."

"So I passed," Tim said.

"Absolutely. With your help, we might catch the bad guy. And you could get a front page scoop for your paper." Andrea went on to explain about the man in disguise she had seen at Plum's. She finished by saying she might have figured out who the man was.

Tim narrowed his brows and looked at Andrea quizzically. "So why don't you just call Oster and wash your hands of this whole thing? You have nothing at stake here."

"Barb has been one of my best friends for a long time," Andrea said frankly. "When it comes to social skills and navigating truth and lies, the twins have the mental ability of young children. It makes me sick and angry that someone would take advantage of them." She paused. "And this new woman in town, who inherited the old Christiansen's Department Store on Main Street? She and I have become friends."

Tim glanced back at Hallie. He seemed almost surprised to find her there. She was playing the wallflower well, apparently.

"You want to pay this guy a visit," Tim said to both the women.

Hallie stepped forward from her place against the wall. "Andrea has this hunch he's involved, and I have to do something. If we went over there—"

"We?" Tim gave a laugh.

Andrea blushed slightly. "I could see for sure that it's him. And we could see what there is to see."

Tim gave her a long, teasing look. "And you want a big, tough guy to go with you," he said. "Let's do it."

Without delay, Tim jumped up and headed for the door. Behind his back, Hallie whispered, "Carpe Diem," reminding Andrea of their earlier conversations about relationships and jumping into the big-girl end of the pool.

Andrea rolled her eyes and mimicked zipping her lips. Together, they headed out the door to meet Tim. A thick snow had begun to fall.

34

Flash had been holed up in his rented trailer for three days now, not daring to show his face around town. All he'd wanted to do was ruin the Christmas trees and force the Greathouses to give up the farm. He only wanted what was rightfully his. He'd never wanted to attract the kind of attention the crime was getting from the statewide news media. And he was getting tired of hiding away, ordering pizza every day. He quickly found out that in Tippy Canoe, the options for ordering-in were severely limited.

If I just wait out the storm a little, things will quiet down, he thought, reviewing his plan for the thousandth time. *Then I can call a real estate agent, make a lowball offer on the land, sell the place for a huge profit, and start a new life.*

His luck had to be more than coincidence. Flash was sure. What were the odds that, only hours before being laid off from the Blue Moon Mine, he'd overheard a conversation between two managers about the urgent need for a landfill? The conversation about needing to hire a company to create a special landfill for mine tailings hadn't made a lot of sense at the time—until later that afternoon. That's when all the employees had been told their jobs were gone—that, as of that moment, the mine was defunct. Out of business.

Asking around over the next couple of days, Flash had learned that the federal government wouldn't let the owners just walk away from the mine, leaving it abandoned. Owners would face jail time unless they used state-required bond money to do an environmental cleanup on the mine site.

And that, Flash had learned, meant finding someone to create a special sealed landfill where the hazardous mercury and arsenic-laden mine tailings could be stored safely underground forever. But federal guidelines were unbending about where the landfill could be located—a certain distance from any river or spring, rain or snow drainage; or natural flood plain or wash areas.

He had scoured the land maps at the county surveyor's office. The only feasible location for the mine-waste landfill was the Christmas tree farm.

This landfill opportunity was a once-in-a-lifetime chance. He knew that. He'd been afraid someone else would learn what he'd learned, and in his panic, he'd done something stupid.

He had contacted the mine owners and told them he understood they needed a large parcel of land fitting the federal requirements for a mine-waste landfill. He happened to own such a piece of land, he'd lied, and he was willing to sell it.

And it had almost been true. The tree farm had been scheduled for a county tax lien option because Lyle Greathouse had fallen behind on his taxes. But at the last minute, the land parcel had been removed from the sale because Marc Greathouse had posted the money needed to pay off the back taxes, penalties, and fees.

And the mayor had snatched Flash's fortune from his fingers, forcing him to take drastic measures. Wherever Marc had gotten the money, Flash would ensure his lenders could clearly see that without income from the sale of trees, there would be no way for Marc to pay the money back.

There was a knock at the door. Finally, his pizza was here. He was ready to eat. Then maybe he'd think about which real estate agent to work with to make his offer for the ruined farm—and just how little money Lyle and Marc Greathouse would be forced to accept for the land.

He staggered to the door, the last four beers taking effect. He opened the door to find a blurry woman with long, ginger hair standing on his stoop. It was tough to see clearly, since he was wearing his sunglasses to keep the lamp's glare from giving him a blinding headache. But he could see she wasn't holding a pizza. She was pretty nice to look at, even with the double vision, though she was using crutches and had a cast on her leg. Maybe he should just haul her inside for a little visit.

Then he noticed the man standing behind her.

"Good evening!" the woman said, her voice too loud and cheerful. "We're with the *Creekside Ledger-Register*, and we're in your neighborhood today with an unbeatable, limited-time subscription offer—"

"Not interested," Flash said harshly. "Now scram." And he slammed the door.

35

Hallie waited in the warmth of Tim's SUV for her two companions to return. Since Hallie had been implicated in the email, both Tim and Andrea thought the man might recognize her. So they had banished her to the car.

Might as well make herself useful.

She looked around the interior to see if she could pick up any clues about the reporter. No kids' seats. But a possible caffeine addict, if the empty Styrofoam cups that littered the backseat were any indication.

She was about to search through the glove box when a rap on the window caught Hallie's attention. Tim opened the door and helped Hallie step out into the wet slush.

"That was definitely him," Andrea whispered to Hallie and Tim. "He was wearing the same sunglasses. Smelled like a liquor store too. Still living in the same trailer he rents from his mother since Judy tossed his sorry behind on the street years ago."

"Judy? Our Judy? Buffalo-chips-and-beehive Judy?" Hallie asked incredulously.

"Yes. The sorry excuse for a human being inside that tin can is

Kenny 'Flask' Petrolo. He used to insist everyone call him 'Flash' for some reason. But since he always walks around between the eternal state of inebriated and hung over, we all started calling him 'Flask.' Between catting around, boozing, and his get-rich-quick schemes, he almost bankrupted Judy and the stores before she got the divorce." Andrea shook her head sadly. "Poor Judy and her boys. Even though they have nothing do with him anymore, it's going to be hard to hear that a member of their family is capable of even worse things than you thought."

"Poor Judy" was right. It was hard to believe that such a vivacious woman had such a large albatross hanging around her neck.

"I hate to be the voice of reason, but just because the man is a lowlife and a drunkard, that doesn't make him a vandal," Tim said.

"Well, let's find something that does," Hallie answered.

She looked around carefully, trying to take in every detail, hoping to find some evidence that he'd been involved in the crime. Andrea said she hadn't been able to see much of the inside of the trailer before the guy slammed the door in their faces. There wasn't much to see on the small stoop, either—a few beer cans and a small, rusty barbecue grill. But even those were just outlines. Snow had been falling for less than fifteen minutes, but it was already covering everything with a blanket of white.

Tim stood guard while Andrea and Hallie walked by Kenny's rickety truck. It was muddy and icy around the wheel wells, but that wouldn't prove anything—not during winter in Tippy Canoe. Hallie desperately wanted to see inside the truck, in case there was a pine-strewn chain saw or some other obvious clue sitting on the front seat. But Mother Nature, as usual, wasn't working in her favor. The thick snow obscured the windows completely. And the bed of the truck was empty, almost as if mocking her.

The trio decided that they should head back into town and decide what to do next before the snow trapped them practically on the bad guy's front porch. Starting the car, Tim began to pull away from the trailer.

As the car moved, something caught Andrea's eye, and she yelled at Tim to stop the car.

"Tim," she said, bouncing up and down in her seat. "We have to find Lieutenant Oster. We've just found the man who hired the Deans to ruin the tree farm."

36

A short time after Flash had slammed the door on the annoying woman trying to sell him a newspaper subscription, there was another knock at the door.

Finally. The pizza.

But this time, there were two sheriff's deputies standing on his stoop.

"Good evening, Kenny," one of the deputies said. He was wearing a badge with the name Lieutenant Damon Oster. "How're we doing tonight?"

Kenny blanched, his confident alter ego evaporating. *Keep cool, keep cool,* he said to himself, trying to keep the panic pounding in his heart from showing on his face. What did they have on him? They must suspect something, somehow, or they wouldn't be here. "Just fine, officers. Waiting for a pizza, actually. Have I done something wrong I should know about?"

"I'm not sure," Oster said. "If you wouldn't mind us coming in for a moment, there are a few questions we'd like to ask you."

Kenny could hardly breathe. It was snowing heavily now, some of it even blowing in the door. If he refused to let them in, he'd seem suspicious. And they might leave for a moment, but they'd be back, and probably with a search warrant. If he let them in, was there anything they might see that he didn't want to be seen? Kenny wracked his brain, giving the room a quick scan, mentally noting the unregistered gun in a bag back in his bedroom. Even as he did, he could see the officers surveying the room from the door, waiting expectantly to see what Kenny would do.

"I've got no problem with that," Kenny said, smiling widely—trying his hardest to seem relaxed and at ease. "I've got nothing to hide from two fine officers of the law."

The deputies stepped inside, searching the room with their eyes.

"That your truck parked out there?" the other deputy said. Even with blurry vision through his sunglasses, Kenny could now see the man was Deputy Lyle Greathouse.

"Yes. Did I do something wrong? The truck is registered and legal and everything, as far as I know."

"You're the registered owner?" Lyle was doing the questioning while Damon took a walk around the room, looking to see what he could see.

"Yeah."

"How long you had it?"

"Seven, eight years, I guess. Got it after that witch took my good one." Kenny paused, deciding it would be okay to show a little annoyance with the visit. "You wanna tell me what's this all about?"

"We've had a report of suspicious behavior," Lyle said enigmatically. "It would sure help us out if we could ask you a few questions. Could I get you to come outside with me to take a look at your truck?"

"It's snowing out there," Kenny said, looking for any excuse.

"I think we'll be okay for a couple of minutes in the snow." Lyle narrowed his eyes, looking deeper at Kenny.

Turning away so as not to let the deputy see any of the dark thoughts hidden behind his eyes, Kenny grumbled, "Let me put some shoes and a coat on."

"You won't mind if I check out your coat and shoes first," Damon said, halting him in mid grab. And then, he followed, "You got any guns or weapons on you? Or in this house?"

"No, sir," Kenny said, sweating just a little. "I don't like violence of any kind. Don't even hunt anymore. My stuff's over there if you want it." He gestured to the end of the hall, where his coat and shoes had been sitting since he'd cleaned them meticulously after returning from the tree farm. He was no dummy. He watched those crime shows on TV.

After deciding the coat and shoes were safe, the three men went outside together. That's when Kenny noticed another vehicle waiting, with three people inside.

"What's going on here?" he asked.

"We've asked someone to come over as a possible witness of stolen property," Damon said.

"I ain't got no stolen property," Kenny said, trying to play the part of the dumb town drunk—not the criminal genius that he knew himself to be. He knew he should be angry, but he was flooded with relief. They really weren't here about the tree farm. They actually thought he might have stolen the truck. It was almost laughable—almost. But he did begin to relax, his internal bravado returning.

Until Damon motioned to the waiting vehicle. The car doors opened, and three people got out. Through the slanting snow, Kenny recognized the saleswoman with the crutches, the man that had been with her, and that blasted California fat cat.

Kenny froze. "Hey, what's this all about? Is this some kind of sting operation? I haven't done anything."

"You know these people?" Lyle asked, his expression blank.

"They were just here not ten minutes ago trying to sell me a newspaper," Kenny growled. "I told 'em to get off my property."

Newspaper . . . maybe this was just about the letter. Maybe

they'd traced it back to him somehow. He thought frantically to everything he'd learned about tracing emails from that one TV show on Thursdays.

"We've asked them to come here to take a look at your truck," Oster said, guiding Kenny to the passenger's side of the truck. And then, pointing to the door, he asked, "Can you tell us what this is? And where you got it?"

Out of the bottom of the passenger's side door was sticking about two inches of—something. Kenny didn't recognize it immediately. Bending closer, he saw the end of a yellow-and-black scarf.

The Deans had each been wearing a yellow-and-black scarf the night they worked with him at the Christmas tree farm. Kenny remembered thinking how ugly the scarves were.

"It looks like a scarf," he said. "I'm not sure where it came from. One of my drinking buddies must have left it."

"How about you open the truck and let us get a look at it."

Kenny already regretted that he'd decided to let the deputies into his house. There was no way he was going to open the truck.

"I don't think I'd like to do that," Kenny said. "I don't know what's going on here, but I don't like it. You people are trying to frame me for something."

"This woman says this scarf belongs to her," Lieutenant Oster said, turning to the crutched woman. "Or rather, it used to belong to her. She made it and another one just like it as Christmas gifts for Lyman and Lehman Dean. Do you know Lyman and Lehman Dean?"

"Never heard of them," Kenny said quickly, his heartbeat going from zero to sixty like a Ferrari. "You're . . . you're barking up the wrong tree." Kenny turned and stomped a few steps back to the safety of his trailer.

"That's funny, because the Deans said they might know you. They told us that someone with a truck just like this one hired them to saw all the trees on Mayor Marc Greathouse's Christmas tree farm," the California woman hollered after him.

Deputy Lyle Greathouse started losing his cool, turning a shade of purple. "My son. My family farm."

"Look, I don't know what you're talking about," Kenny said, lacing his voice in anger in an attempt to deflect some of Lyle's fury. "It's snowing, I'm freezing, and you guys are trying to snoop around in the wrong guy's truck. I haven't done anything, and I'm going to go back inside now, if it's all the same to you fellows."

"Whoa! Slow down," Deputy Greathouse said, getting in Kenny's face. "This woman says this scarf doesn't belong to you. If you can't tell us where this scarf came from, I'm afraid we might have to take you in to ask you a few questions."

"That scarf could belong to anyone," Kenny spat, tempted to shove the deputy out of his space. "Just because you see a yellow-and-black scarf doesn't mean it's the one she made to give someone."

"Actually, that's my scarf. And I can prove it," said the crutch-wielding woman.

When she reached down and brushed the snow off the scarf, at first glance it seemed like any other that Kenny had seen in Walmart or the drug store. But then, when she turned over the knitting, he saw it. A personalized label. Squinting, he could just make it out, once his vision had stopped moving—"Handcrafted for you with loving care by Andrea Linford."

Lieutenant Damon Oster, shining his flashlight on the tag, read it aloud.

Kenny knew he had not a moment to lose before possibly being arrested. He had only one trick left up his sleeve—he had to try buying time by intimidating these small-town cops with big words.

"That explains everything. A clear conspiracy," Kenny lied. "I noticed this woman fiddling around near my truck a few minutes ago when they came here the first time. I saw her out the window. She must have planted that scarf. She trespassed on my property.

She lied about being here to sell me a newspaper subscription." He looked at the three from the car now. "I don't know who you are, or what you are trying to do, but I'm calling my lawyer. Something illegal is going down here. Officers, was it legal for her to sneak onto my property without permission and touch my truck?"

"We didn't touch anything," the city girl protested.

"Officers, arrest these people for tampering with my truck, for breaking and entering, and for trespassing on private property," Kenny commanded. "And I'm calling my lawyer, right now." He looked at the two officers sternly. "You got a problem with that? Can a man call his attorney when he is being falsely accused?"

Lieutenant Ostler looked at Deputy Greathouse.

"Get your attorney on the phone," Deputy Greathouse said, sighing. "We do have some questions for you, and you have the right to have your attorney present."

Kenny Petrolo stomped into his trailer, muttering obscenities.

Once inside, Flash, his alter-ego and mastermind, reemerged. He knew the clock was ticking. He shoved clothes into a bag and grabbed his wallet and gun. In less than a minute, he was silently slipping out the back door of the trailer and getting onto the paved road behind the house. He ran through the snow still melting on the wet road so he wouldn't leave any tracks.

37

It had been a long night, and Hallie didn't make it back to her room until 11:00 p.m. The next day, outside her hotel room door, was the paper—just like it had been every other day. Except today, Tim Brotherton's coverage of all that had transpired in Tippy Canoe was on the front page of the *Bozeman Daily Chronicle*. The headline read: "Suspect in Christmas Tree Vandalism Escapes Police."

A former employee of the now-defunct Blue Moon Silver Mine escaped on foot after police attempted to question him regarding the destruction of a local Christmas tree farm.

The farm belongs to the family of Tippy Canoe Mayor Marc Greathouse. Kenny Petrolo, 37, was about to be arrested after being confronted by police in his home. Police had received a tip from a local resident about evidence of the tree farm crime in Petrolo's truck, according to Sheriff's Office Lieutenant Damon Oster. Police declined to comment on the nature of the evidence in the truck but did confirm to the *Bozeman Daily Chronicle* that the truck has been impounded.

"We have reason to believe that Kenny Petrolo attempted to frame both Mayor Marc Greathouse and business owner Hallie Stone in a bizarre, poison pen letter," said Oster in an interview. "Because there have been no reports of stolen vehicles, we believe suspect Kenny Petrolo, who has been known to use the alias Flash, is still in Tippy Canoe. We have issued a warrant for his arrest, and we are asking anyone who might have information about Mr. Petrolo's whereabouts to come forward."

In a bizarre twist, when reached for comment, Mayor Greathouse said he had considered secretly taking $35,000 from city coffers.

Greathouse said he needs the cash to pay a tax lien on his father's farm, which has been in the family for four generations. The *Chronicle* has obtained documents confirming that, at one point, Greathouse transferred $35,000 from a city account to his own personal account, but transferred the money back to the city less than twenty-four hours later. In an interview, the mayor apologized for what he called a momentary lapse in judgment. He said he has no plans to resign.

"I was unaware that the taxes on the farm were delinquent," said Greathouse. "When this came to my attention, I knew our family would be able to pay the tax bill in full as soon as the Christmas tree sale was finished. But the lien deadline fell before our annual Christmas tree sale. In my panic, I thought about borrowing money from the city for a few days. My plan was to pay back the city in full, and with interest."

The mayor said that he soon realized the folly of his plan. He decided on his own to return the money to the city and try to find another way to save the family farm. The Greathouse family Christmas tree farm is still scheduled to appear in a county tax lien property auction in less than one week.

"Because vandals have destroyed the Christmas trees, we expect to lose the farm," said Greathouse. "My father and I are exploring our options and hoping for a miracle."

Hallie searched through the rest of the paper for any more information. She hardly slept last night with the thought of that creep running loose. Maybe she would luck out and find a notice of a suspicious sighting of him . . . in Florida.

Rifling through the pages, she did find a second article about Tippy Canoe. Though the news piece was somewhat hidden in the newspaper's Life & Style section, it was coverage of the town's good parts too. A short sidebar story announced that, despite the political drama, the Christmas Cave Festival had already doubled the number of visitors to the town. Shop owners were quoted as saying the festival was a godsend for the town's struggling economy. Their article even mentioned that part-time Sheriff Deputy Lyle Greathouse had begun offering hay-wagon rides along Main Street to any visitor who made a donation toward future improvements to the cave's visitor center.

Hallie was pleased that the free advertising idea had paid off, even if it was not in the way they originally intended. And the wagon rides were a nice touch. She hadn't thought about offering anything like that, but it was a great idea. She would definitely make sure to stop by. Sometime.

Aside from Andrea, Tim, and the deputies, she hadn't seen anyone else since last night. It was well into the afternoon now. Afraid to face the town's active rumor mill, she had hidden herself away.

Partly, she worried people would look at her differently.

That scene in Plum's Pantry had been nightmare inducing—even though it eventually worked out. To be the target of so much suspicion and dislike, even briefly, had been extremely painful.

Hallie wondered how Barb would look at her now that everything had been sorted out. Would she feel bad about calling Hallie the devil incarnate? Or would she still blame Hallie for the whole mess anyway?

And what about Marc? That momentary look on his face at Plum's had been one of betrayal. It was clear that, at least for a moment, he had thought she was some California drug lord out to ruin his life.

Before this mess, Hallie had started thinking that there might just be . . . something. A connection between her and the mayor. Maybe she had put too much stock into those looks that they shared in the cave. After all, she was still an outsider in this tight-knit community, and he had no reason to trust her. At least his mistrust had only lasted a second before he fiercely defended her to Barb, Ula, and the rest of crowd. Knowing that didn't really stop the sting though, and it made her hesitant to put herself out there again.

But there was more bothering her than that. Even more than the fact that there was a psycho on the loose. The adrenaline of yesterday had faded, and now that the mystery was solved, Hallie was left remembering why she was here in the first place. Being here, in this place where Finn had made a new home for himself, was unsettling. It opened doors in her heart that she thought were long closed. How could she figure out how she felt about Marc when she didn't know how she felt about Finn?

More than a week had passed since Hallie arrived in Tippy Canoe. And though plenty had happened, she was no closer to finding a buyer for her inheritance. But at least Kobold's was no longer shuttered. Melora had agreed to open the shop while the festival was going on.

Hallie paused over her coffee, knowing she had some decisions to make. Her original plan had been to sell the business and leave, never to return to Montana. But after being here, she was rethinking that plan. She didn't want to sell off Christiansen's and leave everyone's fate in the hands of some business person. She also couldn't move here permanently, abandoning her California studio on the beach. That was obviously out of the question—the sun and surf were her home. But there was a third option that seemed to be growing more attractive all the time. If she decided not to sell Christiansen's, she could have a second home that could serve as an escape from the LA traffic, tension, and smog.

She never expected the rustic, village-like atmosphere in Tippy Canoe to appeal to her; she was a born-and-bred city girl. The great outdoors was what you watched on the National Geographic channel from the comfort of your couch. But there was something to be said for being able to see great swathes of stars in the night sky and hear birdsong fill the silence. And for being greeted by friendly faces wherever she went, with a few minor exceptions.

I could see myself coming here a few times a year to paint and relax, she thought. After she was done with the Venice series, she imagined moving from cityscapes to something more natural. There was a calm here that was unexpected and penetrated deep. It filled a hole that she didn't know she'd had. There were definite possibilities for growth in both her professional life—and her personal one. A sly grin snuck across her face. And it didn't hurt that there was a ruggedly handsome man around who might be willing to help explore both of those.

Thinking of Marc—thinking of her love life, or lack thereof, in general—reminded Hallie that there was unfinished business, a task both physical and emotional that she had to face before leaving for California.

How had Andrea put it?

Cleaning out the refrigerator.

They were going to pay. *They were all going to pay.* His dreams had been so close and then ripped from his grasp. He threw the newspaper into the fire pit. Hallie Stone and Marc Greathouse. Right there in the black and white print. Clearly, they were to blame for fate getting offtrack.

Well, they weren't going to get away with it. First, he'd start with the outsider. The warmth of the flames ignited his imagination. He was going to send a message to this town that had never shown him the respect he deserved. The town that had ridiculed him, laid him off, promised him wealth, then tried to put him in jail forever.

He needed a place to hide out and put his plan in motion. He knew just the place where no one would think to look for him.

Staring in to the flames, he knew just what to do.

Flash was back.

39

Marc had gone over to Plum's for a bite but was surprised to see Andrea out after her long night of chasing down villains. Even though Kenny had escaped, Marc owed Andrea a great deal of thanks. It was a little awkward, though, now that the whole town knew about his ill-attempted creative financing. Hoping to clear the air one or two folk at a time, he sat next to Andrea at her table. She was in mid-conversation with Barb.

"Lieutenant Oster says no charges will be filed against the boys for what they did," Barb said. "Lyle told me he has no desire to press charges against the twins because he knows they were duped by that man. Myself, I'd still like to have just a minute's chance to take Kenny Petrolo by the throat for what he's put us through—not just me and the boys, but the whole town. I hope they catch him soon."

Marc was about to second his dad's opinion about the twins and express his long-standing dislike of Kenny when he heard the voice of Ula Blackboro.

"I saw there was a party here and decided to pop in," she said.

Ula's voice was cheerful as always, but Marc noticed the old bird's expression was grave.

"I know what's on your mind," Andrea said. "Tippy Canoe Academy."

"For a few minutes yesterday, I had believed we could save the school through donations from the alumni," Ula said sadly. "Now I realize the idea probably wasn't realistic even then." She gave Marc a stern, reproachful look. "And since you couldn't resist sticking your hand in the city's honey pot, I'm sure we won't see another penny in donations. Only a fool would send money our way now."

Marc hadn't thought it was possible to sink any lower. He was wrong. Not only was the family farm about to be practically given away by Uncle Sam, but Bob and Betty were starting to talk retirement with their beloved greenhouses about to be gone. Now he could add the fate of Tippy Canoe Academy to his list of casualties.

Maybe he should rethink resigning. Clearly, he was the worst mayor ever. Shoot, he was probably the worst man too. Aside from that drunk Kenny, that is.

"Truth be told," Ula said, interrupting the gloomy silence, "I was hoping you all could help me. I'm not ready to play dead to Tidewater just because of a bad decision."

"In a few days, the kids will be out for the Christmas school break," Andrea said. "As much as I agree with you about playing dead, I also worry about them. A lot of them must already be feeling the uncertainty, and I think it could be hard on them to spend the whole Christmas break unsure of where they will be going to school in January, who their teachers will be, and whether they will like their new classes."

"On the other hand, think of the bus ride from here to Meagher County," Barb said, shuddering. "I was bused to school as a child. Those kids will have to be on a bus for forty or fifty minutes every morning, and the same after school. They'll have to get up earlier.

They'll get home later. And school buses can be one of the most toxic atmospheres on the planet—a real Lord-of-the-Flies situation. If my twins had had to ride the bus every day instead of walk, well . . ." Her voice trailed. "That just never would have worked, that's all. I think you're right, Ula. Our kids deserve the academy. And we should fight for them."

"I hadn't considered the whole bus situation," Andrea said, nodding.

"And no one in Tippy Canoe is going to have a relaxed, restful holiday with this hanging over the town," Ula said, her wrinkles deepening. "Problem is, we need a solution. Double-time! And I've got no ideas. I thought maybe if we talked it through, maybe we could—"

"Come up with something," Barb said.

They were all silent for a length, lost in thought.

"So much for talking it through," Andrea said with a laugh.

Marc still felt uncertain about his place—his role—now that his flaws were laid bare. But still, he had an idea. "Okay, well, there is that old saying—the enemy of my enemy is my friend. Who are Tidewater's enemies on this whole budget-cut issue?"

"Wow," Andrea said, the first to warm to Marc's presence, if only slightly. "The enemy of my enemy is my friend. I like it. By that logic, I guess we could say the whole state is Tidewater's enemy. Everyone wants smaller class sizes, and none of us want to pay more taxes."

"It's parents and voters in the overcrowded districts that are pressuring Tidewater," Ula said, actually speaking to Marc rather than at him like before. "They think closing the smaller, rural schools will free up money to spend in their districts."

"Ula, you said something at the press conference that I thought was true," Marc said, growing more confidant. "If our students in the academy are scoring better grade point averages, it seems illogical to close the better performing school in an attempt to throw more money at the underperforming schools."

"Hey, wait just a stinkin' minute," Andrea said. "That's a great point. Why should we punish our students by sending them to a *lower-performing school system?* You'd think it would be the other way 'round. You'd think they'd be wanting to send their kids over to us."

"Heaven forbid," Barb groaned, feigning a grimace. "Just what we need—them sending all their delinquents our way."

"Wait a minute, though," Ula said, suddenly perking up. "That's just the thing. We don't want their delinquents, that's true. But what if we take their better students? We shouldn't be closing our school. We should be opening it to their best students. I mean, we have a lot to offer—smaller class sizes, far fewer discipline problems, a better success rate in our advanced-prep classes. I'll bet our percentage of graduating seniors receiving college scholarships beats theirs hands down."

"But how would we make sure we were getting the wheat and not the chafe too?" Barb asked, looking worried.

"I'd need to check out the legality since we are a state school, but we'd make rules," Marc said, his enthusiasm growing. "We'd set minimum requirements for any transfer students—a minimum grade-point average, and no one with attendance problems or a juvenile record."

"We could cap transfers at a certain number," Ula said, growing warmer and more cheerful with each exchange. "It's perfect. The academy has room for probably more than a third or half as many students as we have there now. And the state divvies out a certain amount of money per pupil—"

"So if we can draw off some of the cream of their crop, so to speak, the state will not only have to keep the academy open but send us more money too," Marc pointed out.

"Instead of forcing the better school to close its doors . . ." Andrea began.

"The Meagher school system is forced to compete," Ula finished.

"Wait a second, though," Barb said, suddenly crestfallen. "There's a fly in our ointment. No one from Meagher is going to want to drive their kids all the way to Tippy Canoe, even if our school is better."

Silence.

"Some might," Andrea offered weakly.

"In the winter? Would you have let Megan drive to Meagher every morning on the winter roads?"

"Okay, okay. You've got me there."

"Wait." Marc stood up and paced for a moment, allowing his idea to finish forming. "Fair is fair, right? If the state is willing to pay to bus our kids to Meagher, they can't very well refuse to bus Meagher to us. Especially if we get enough parents to sign their kids up for the transfer. The state will have to dig into the tight pockets for a bus."

Ula clapped Marc on the back with a strength belying her far-advanced age. "Good on you, boy. I knew you were worth keeping around after all."

Marc was sure he was beaming from the inside out, having won over one of the town's most curmudgeony residents. Perhaps there was still a little place in the town for him yet.

"So we need to start getting Meagher parents excited about sending their kids to the academy, pronto," Andrea said. "How're we going to pull that off?"

Ula smiled. "Time for another press conference."

40

TIPPY CANOE TAKES ON TIDEWATER; RESIDENTS REFUSE TO CLOSE ACADEMY—that was the headline Marc and Ula put on the press release to all the media. If Marc had learned any lesson from recent events, it was this: the secret of getting the media's attention was for residents to get involved—the media are drawn to people with pep and a few good sound-bite quotes.

Then again, nearly all the media was still hanging around to cover the escape—still waiting around to see what other little news nuggets the "quirky" town of Tippy Canoe would provide.

Marc wanted to make sure that the town's residents wouldn't disappoint.

This time, Marc asked Tippy Canoe parents to take the lead—under Ula's direct supervision, of course. Melora and David Post of Cracked Rock and their two children; Peter Tumpi, his wife, Isabel, and their three daughters; Matt Teasdale, an adjunct music teacher, and his very pregnant wife Brooklyn, owners of "His" and "Her"—all these and more had shown up to show the state their determination to keep the academy open. Andrea was showing her support by covering the story from press corps seating. In fact, to Marc's eyes, it seemed most if not all of the 135 academy students were here with their families.

One noticeable absence was Judy and her sons—sixteen-year-old Dominic and thirteen-year-old Kenny Jr. After the news broke that Judy's ex-husband was responsible for the tree vandalism, reporters and lookey-loos had been parked all down her street. Understandably, she was keeping a low profile. Poor woman didn't deserve to suffer. Just one more thing to put at that slimeball's door whenever he was tracked down. And Kenny had better be praying it wasn't Marc that did the finding.

A light snow was falling outside, so today's announcement was being held inside the academy's multi-purpose room, St. Joer Hall. Marc wanted to make sure that today's headline was all about the school and not his own family drama. So he stayed away from the press's view and orchestrated some of the finer points behind the scenes. By arrangement, Matt Teasdale opened the meeting.

"We're here today to make a special announcement. But before we get to that, let us quickly summarize what Tippy Canoe Academy is up against," Matt said. "We understand the state is in a budget crunch. We understand that belts must be tightened. We understand and advocate fiscal prudence. We know our neighbors, the parents of children in the Meagher County School System, have been vocal about their desire to see their schools improved."

"What we cannot understand is this," David Post said, joining Matt at the podium. "Why would Governor Tidewater be pushing the state board of education officials to close the school with the highest per-pupil grade-point average? Why close the school that consistently has a nearly one-hundred percent pass rate on the advanced placement tests that give college credit to graduating seniors? Why do away with the school with the highest number of graduating seniors receiving college scholarships? The school with the lowest student-teacher ratio?

"And why shutter the school that has one of the lowest, if not the very lowest, rate of disciplinary-action incidents?" Matt said.

"The bureaucrats see force as that answer. They want to compel Tippy Canoe Academy, with its truly stellar academic record, to close so they can spend the academy's budget in Meagher County. That's the bureaucratic solution. We have a different plan. A common sense plan."

"We see choice, not force, as the answer," Melora said, joining them and taking over. "Tippy Canoe Academy would like to extend a special invitation. For a short time, on a first-come, first-serve basis, the academy will offer an open enrollment for certain academically qualified students. To put it in more everyday words, by almost any measure, the academy is turning out the best students in the state. If you are the parent of a hard-working student, we invite you to consider whether the academy might be the best place for your child's education."

The catch, of course, was the distance, the trio went on to explain. True, students coming from Meagher County would need to travel to the academy and back each day. But for some students, especially those academically successful students who were struggling as small fish in the big pond that was the Meagher County system, the bus ride might well be the ticket to a better future.

Two decades before, the academy had been full with just over 180 students, the parents explained. As Tippy Canoe's population had leveled off and aged, attendance had dropped, leaving space for two additional classes of twenty students each. Any parent wishing to transfer their child was advised to act quickly.

"Once those forty slots are filled, enrollment will be closed again," Matt said. "In order to keep the integrity of the academy, and the sharp academic focus we have grown to expect, we've made a decision that the academy will never expand beyond the number of students who attended at its peak twenty years ago. We prefer to keep our class sizes small and retain our small-school atmosphere, where the children are the first priority and internal politics and bureaucratic red tape are not welcome."

"This afternoon, we will be filing a request with the state to provide a daily bus from Meagher County to the academy, for the convenience of parents and families who wish to transfer," Melora said, almost defiantly. "We want to put the state school board on notice: if our bus request is not honored, we will choose to close Tippy Canoe Academy and reopen it as a charter school, with charter funds."

"Either way," Matt concluded, "we want our academy students to know this: when you come back from Christmas vacation, the academy will still be your school. Some students have worried about what might happen. You don't need to worry any more. Tippy Canoe Academy is not closing. Your school will go on and will continue to be one of the top academic performers in the state."

Even from Marc's chosen vantage spot, just in the hallway, away from the media's glare, Ula could be heard shouting, "Put that in your pipe and smoke it, Tidewater."

41

Kobold's was quiet. Melora had already closed up the shop for the day, having something else she needed to do. Hallie knew that, had she asked, Andrea would have happily joined her expedition to Finn's apartment. But she knew what awaited her couldn't be beaten or scared away with a few friends and a baseball bat. The ghosts upstairs were for her alone.

She climbed the stairs at the back of the store, stopping to remember which key Melora told her opened the door. Slipping the key into the lock, the door opened easily.

"Okay, Finn," Hallie nervously said aloud. "I'm here, ready or not."

She was surprised to find the space was modern and strongly resembled the flat they had once shared. Finn had clearly spent some money to have the place updated. There was a good-sized kitchen, a living room, a guest bathroom, and a large master suite. In every room, there were Finn's signature piles—piles of papers, art magazines, art books, junk mail, bills. And just as Andrea had predicted, Finn had a studio. It was toward the back of the building, occupying the portion of the second-floor space with the best windows.

Finn had indeed been painting. It was a relief to know he hadn't changed that piece of himself, at least.

"Let's see what you were up to." Somehow Hallie felt comforted, or at least less alone, speaking aloud to Finn. "Maybe you're even still hanging around here," she said. Then she added, "If you can hear me—or if there is an angel or someone taking messages for you—I just want to say thanks. Thanks for the years you gave me. We were happy for a while there, weren't we? I hope you don't mind me looking at your work. If you do, well, then you should have taken it with you."

Surprisingly, most of what she found in the room were miniature canvases—paintings only a few inches in size. Finn had occasionally experimented with miniatures, Hallie remembered, but it had never been something she'd known him to focus on.

The artwork here showcased his talent for capturing meaning in ordinary details. There were tiny, minimalist horizontal sketches of wilderness—forest scenes, lakes, mountain vistas. And there was a series of views of a single snow-swept tree. Finn had dragged white gesso over a charcoal, bare-limbed tree, giving the impression that the tree was being buffeted by strong winds in a snowstorm. The affect was a stroke of minimalist genius, Hallie thought to herself.

Stacked under one of the windows, Hallie found some larger paintings. She was surprised to see that one of them was a painting of Kobold's basement door, with the arts-and-crafts back plate and blue-green, antique glass knob that Hallie had admired. There was also a painting of the Kobold's storefront. Another, apparently done from memory, showed what Hallie gathered was the entire building as Christiansen's, from when Finn's father had been alive. Perhaps it was even a view from Finn's childhood memories.

"Finn, you should have hung these up downstairs," Hallie said aloud. "They're great. And they honor the spirit of this building." She paused. "I am going to put them up in the shop—like it or lump it." It was one of Finn's vernacular sayings. "If you didn't want the world to see them, you shouldn't have died and left them here for me to find. So there." She laughed to herself. It was just the kind of tongue-in-cheek humor that she and Finn had shared in the happier days of their romance.

While it lasted, theirs had been a good relationship—great even. *You were definitely the love of my life*, thought Hallie. *Maybe I shouldn't have chased the golden egg so much. Maybe I should have put more focus on the people in my life. If only . . .*

Unbidden, tears welled in her eyes. She remembered the terrible day when she'd miscarried. She and Finn had so much wanted to have a child together—and Finn had been so happy when she'd gotten pregnant. And then, one terrible night in the fourth month, cramps had overtaken her, and she'd delivered a small, tumorlike mass into the toilet. The dream was over.

Hallie had spent a week in bed practically comatose and silent. After those seven days, she got up like nothing had happened. She hadn't ever spoken of the miscarriage again. But that night, something had changed. Shutting out the rest of the world, she buried her pain into her work. Slowly, a gap had opened between her and Finn, and increasingly, there was less laughter and more silence.

"I left you behind," she said aloud, realizing the truth of the words.

Hallie's legs lost their strength, and she folded not so gracefully to the floor. Even with her face in her hands, the tears still leaked through her fingers and onto the red oak floor in little droplets.

"Oh Finn. I was so wrong. All this time, I thought you weren't supporting my success, but it was me that didn't support you. We needed to grieve, and I wouldn't let you. I'm sorry. I hope you were able to find happiness here."

As if in answer to her plea, a gust of wind blew from absolutely nowhere, sending the drop cloth in the corner flying. Where had that come from, and why hadn't she seen that corner before?

Underneath the drop cloth was a collection of portraits.

Finn had never dabbled in people. He always claimed he had trouble capturing the essence of the soul beneath the planes of the face.

From the floor, Hallie couldn't tell whether the paintings were his. On hands and knees, she crawled closer to the corner. The closest piece was a portrait of Finn standing next to Kobold's. A look on the bottom left of the canvas confirmed that the artist's signature was indeed Finn's blocky script.

"Well, I'll be darned. You finally got it." And he had. It was not merely a likeness of Finn on the canvas; it was a piece of him. There was life in the eyes and humor in the smile. The colors, the expressions . . . all showed love and life. Were there more?

Hallie was hungry but not for food. Her stomach grumbled. Okay, maybe not just for food, but for more proof that Finn had found solace here. It was important to know that her selfishness hadn't ruined his life. She avidly flipped through every canvas, charcoal, and sketch. It seemed like the whole town had been captured and displayed through Finn's eyes.

The Dean twins were painted, conferring with each other, heads together. No doubt sharing more of their twin speak. There was a great piece that showed Deputy Greathouse with his chest proudly puffed out, star gleaming brightly on his jacket. There was another group picture with all the tenants gathered together in front of Christiansen's. In the portrait, David dwarfed his much smaller wife. But it radiated a fierce protectiveness, something Hallie had noticed on occasion in real life. Finn somehow managed to express the pride she had seen in the Tumpis. They had worked hard to get their slice of the American dream, and you could feel that just looking at them.

Most telling, though, was the way Finn had portrayed beehive Judy. While Hallie had seen a tangled, slightly crazy women, Finn had seen an eccentric piece of art. She looked put together, beautiful, and her whole being seemed to radiate warmth. If this painting and the other three solo portraits of Judy were any indication,

Finn had visited the Frost Shoppe for more than just the Buffalo Chip shake.

Hallie busted out laughing. Judy and Finn would have made a good pair. "You old dog. You really were happy. I thought you tucked your tail and ran away here to hide. Instead, you found something even better."

The hours flew by as Hallie rummaged through all of Finn's things. Everywhere she looked, there was evidence of the man she had loved. But there were also clues into aspects of the man that she had never known. Like the large collection of The Cat Who, Agatha Christie, and Miss Marple novels. Apparently, Phineus was a closet mystery cozy lover. His CD collection included all his old favorites that she remembered, like Grieg and Fresh Aire. But there was also a big section of big band hits. The trumpet next to the stereo seemed to indicate that, at some point, Finn had become a musician as well.

Probably one of the most interesting things was a set of drafting blueprints. Hand-drawn by Finn himself. He had been planning on renovating the basement into two sections. The main area looked like it was structured to be a mini gallery. The darkroom area was reconstructed into a small studio apartment with a separate exterior entrance. It didn't take a genius to figure out who the intended residents were.

The plans were ambitious and amazing. "So now what, huh? What do you expect me to do with these? I wish you had left instructions. Give me a sign; I'm clueless here."

Hallie threw herself down on the leather couch with a thud. A second thud followed immediately after. Poking her head up just enough over the armrest, she could see one of the portraits had fallen over, revealing the painting behind. A portrait of Marc Greathouse.

And just what am I supposed to do with that little tidbit, huh? She remembered Marc saying something about building his own house. Maybe he would have a clue what to do with these plans.

Perhaps Andrea had been on to something. More than just the pain medication, that is. Maybe Andrea's late husband and Finn were both in cahoots, sending messages and constructing events from the great beyond. "Nah," she said, chuckling aloud at the ridiculousness of the thought.

The mystery draft from out of nowhere rose up again. It brought goose bumps to her skin and lifted the hairs on her neck. "Then again, it wouldn't hurt to give the mayor a call and ask him to consult."

Twenty minutes later, Hallie rushed down the stairs when she heard a knock at the shop door. Before opening the door, she took a quick detour through the store aisles to find one of those souvenir Barefoot makeup compacts. Looking back at her reflection, she gave herself the once-over and checked her teeth for stuck food.

Smoothing her hair, she couldn't help feeling self-conscious and a little nervous. *Get yourself together woman*, Hallie mentally chided herself. *It's not like this is a date or anything. Just a man coming over. In the middle of the night. Because you called him. To talk "business."* Her brain could not help but point out the striking similarities to the time in high school when she'd called Carl Benson over to work on "homework."

This is serious, she insisted to herself. She really needed his opinion on the project in the basement. *And it couldn't have waited for the morning sun?* the demon on her shoulder countered.

Hallie chose to plead the fifth on that one.

The knocking resumed a little louder this time, snapping her out of her inner argument.

Hallie jogged to the door, muttering along the way, "Okay, Finn. You'd better know what you're doing. If this blows up in my face, I will hunt you down in the afterlife."

She put on a big smile and jerked open the door.

"I'm sorry. I was . . ." The words died on her lips.

Standing in front of her was a giant Christmas wreath adorned with gauzy, white tulle bows, silver tinsel, and bright red buffalo berries.

The wall of flannel the wreath appeared to be hanging on belonged to none other than her summoned midnight caller, Marc Greathouse.

"I thought the shop could use a bit of Christmas cheer, so I made this for you. I have enough pine boughs from all the ruined trees that I could make a hundred more if you'd like," Marc said as he proudly handed Hallie his creation.

"No, no. Thank you. This one is more than enough. It's . . . lovely."

It was hideous. Clearly Marc had put a lot of work into his thoughtful gift, but to be honest—the man was no Martha Stewart. She hoped he could build a little better than he crafted.

"I also wanted to apologize for believing that venomous letter for even a minute. I should have had more faith. I'm sorry," Marc said, looking for all the world like a scolded and shamed little boy.

Though the rejection had hurt, it was past now, and she wanted to keep things light. "Apology accepted. After all, I can see how easy it would be to confuse me for a drug kingpin. It happens a lot—more than you might think."

Marc perked up at her attempted humor, giving a few courtesy chuckles. "You don't know how relieved that makes me. I was worried you might blame me for getting you involved in my mess."

"You didn't get me involved in anything. It was that evil son of a moose. I think you were very courageous to tell the truth about the city funds."

The room filled with silence at the mention of Marc's almost crime.

"So, um, you're probably wondering why I called you here so late at night," Hallie said, awkwardly changing the subject as she put down the pine monstrosity.

"I'll admit I'm a bit curious as to what kind of business proposition you might have for a disgraced mayor and manager of a now-defunct Christmas tree farm," he said.

"Well, I was going through some of Finn's things, and I came across these plans."

Hallie raised the rolled tube of paper from behind the sales counter. "Blueprints, actually. I thought of you, since you had mentioned you were pretty handy doing construction tasks. They're for the basement; he wanted to . . . well, it's probably easier if we go down and look."

Marc placed a broad hand on her back and gestured grandly toward the stairs to the basement and at the back of the store. "After you, miss."

A warm sensation crept across Hallie's back and up her neck. She walked quickly ahead so that Marc wouldn't see her face growing flushed.

Pretend like your heart didn't just try to leap out through your throat. Say something—anything.

"I didn't get a chance to ask more about the tree farm. Is there any hope?"

"Not a lot," Marc admitted grimly. "The county extended the deadline for an extra week before it goes to auction on account of the whole vandalism thing. But I still have to come up with all the money, and now I don't have a product to sell. Nobody wants a felled or mangled tree." He chuckled and glanced to the front counter where Hallie had deposited his wreath. "Maybe I should make a ton of wreaths just like that and sell them to make up the cash."

Oh dear, Hallie thought as she laughed along with him. *If that's all he's got, he doesn't have a prayer.*

They lapsed into more awkward silence on their way down the stairs. Hallie walked through the craftsman door and searched for a good place to lay out the plans.

Marc broke the stillness first. "So if you're planning on building something, does that mean you're thinking of sticking around for a while?" There was a quality in his tone of voice that Hallie couldn't put her finger on. It almost sounded like . . . hope.

She whirled around too fast so she could see the expression on his face—and whacked Marc with her roll of blueprints, dropping them on the ground. When she went to retrieve them she didn't see the big, red container on the ground. Something sloshed out. Tripping over it, she pitched forward.

Straight into the waiting arms of Marc.

It felt so good to be enfolded in his broad embrace. Hallie could see it all in her head. She would look up at him. He would look at her. They would share a moment. And then, just maybe . . .

But that never happened, because a chilling and dissident bark of laughter from the darkness came.

"Lucky me! It seems I've caught two rats instead of just one in this tourist trap."

43

The smell of spilled gasoline burned at Marc's sinuses.

Kenny glowered at Marc. "I'd planned to deal with our mouse-of-a-mayor later. But since you're here, I might as well deal with you now. You're making this too easy for me." He laughed maniacally.

Marc knew Kenny as Judy's ex and as an all-around bum, but he also knew him from the Blue Moon Mine. They had never worked directly together: Marc didn't even remember ever having a conversation with Kenny. But Marc did remember the rumors. A couple of times, Kenny had been accused of stealing thousands of dollars of expensive tools and petty cash that mysterious disappeared. But no one had ever been able to prove anything. Kenny had been mostly known on the job for his chronic laziness, snarly attitude, and aloofness.

Laughing too loudly, almost nervously, Kenny pulled a pistol out of his jacket and pointed it at nowhere in particular—yet.

"All I'd wanted to do was ruin the Christmas trees and force you, Mayor, to give up your cockeyed Christmas farm. That land should have been mine! I was the one who was smart. I was the one who figured out that your wannabe field of firewood was actually worth something! It was the only land in the county that fit the Fed's long list of requirements to store the crap tailings from the Blue Moon. You should have walked away after we mangled your precious trees. You might have royally screwed me over, but if I ain't getting the money, you ain't getting it either, pal."

A chill settled over Marc. This guy wasn't kidding around. Marc and Hallie needed to get out of here, and fast. What were their chances of making it up the stairs before Kenny could get off a shot?

Kenny turned to Hallie. "You, with your ridiculous shoes and business suits. You should have stayed in the city and kept your nose out of our little town." He looked at her menacingly. "But this is gonna be your town now. Your new forever-home. *Because this is where you're gonna be buried.*"

He leveled his pistol at her head. He motioned toward the darkroom. "Both of you, get back there."

Marc looked at Hallie. Hallie met his eyes, narrowing her own. There was fear in her eyes. But there was also something else. She was trying to tell him something, trying to relay a message.

She quickly glanced at Kenny and then looked back, for one long last second, at Marc.

Clearly, she had a plan. Marc gave a slight nod of his head. So far, Hallie had proven herself to be one resourceful woman. He was ready to follow her lead.

Hallie looked Kenny square in the eyes. "So, is your plan to burn us along with the building?"

Kenny smiled wickedly, though slightly off kilter. "I'm not *really* evil. I'd never burn someone to death. I'll shoot you first. Just to be nice."

Hallie did not look away. "So, you want the building to explode—with you in it too, Kenny?"

"It's Flash!" he yelled, irritated. He continued a little more calmly but still looked crazy. "I'm the Flash, and my fiery friend would never hurt me."

"It will if you shoot and hit the propane tank."

Marc looked at Hallie. No one kept propane tanks inside a building. Where was she going with this?

Kenny's bravado seemed to slip a notch. "What tank? I haven't seen a propane tank."

"Over there." Hallie pointed toward the ragged curtains leading into the darkroom.

As Kenny looked at the darkroom, Hallie gave Marc a look and a jerk of her head.

Marc got the message. He charged at Kenny, tackling the man at full force.

Everything became a blur. Kenny whirled around at the last second, and the gun discharged as both men went down. Blinding pain ran across Marc's temple before he went numb.

Hallie screamed and lunged at Marc. The force of Marc's tackle had knocked Kenny backward, slamming his head onto the concrete floor with a sickening thud. Blood poured from Marc's head, obscuring his vision. He landed on top of Kenny, and the gun went off again.

At the same time, the spark from the ricocheting bullet lit the gasoline. The basement erupted in a blaze.

44

Smoke started to billow as the curtains from the darkroom burst into flames. Kenny looked like he was down for the count, and Marc was bleeding profusely from the head.

Hallie ran over to them, praying to anyone who was listening for Marc to still be alive. There was so much blood. Kneeling over Marc, she could see just the barest of movement with the rise and fall of his chest.

He was alive.

But he wouldn't be for long unless she could get them out before the fire spread. She tugged on Marc's arm in a futile attempt to drag him to the door. Hallie coughed, choking back the acrid smoke filling up the room. Her plan was obviously going nowhere. And she was running out of time.

She gave one last shove, but Marc had to weigh at least two hundred pounds. Kenny groaned from underneath Marc, almost as if to say he thought Marc was pretty heavy too.

Now what? Both men were still alive, but neither one was in any condition to be of any help. It was up to her to save them all. And she did mean *all*. Because even if she could somehow manage to pull Marc out of the basement, her conscience would not allow her to leave the other man to die. Even a man as wicked as Kenny.

If she couldn't get them away from the fire, she was going to have to get the fire away from them. Hallie boldly ran toward the flaming curtains and ripped them to the ground. She jumped and stomped, using her "ridiculous shoes" to help smother the flames. Unfortunately, the fire had begun to spread along the wood accents that she had admired only days before. Now she cursed them.

She looked around the floor for something, anything that she could use. The curtains were only bits of ash now, and she needed something like a blanket. Or . . .

A sleeping bag.

There on the floor in the darkroom were the two sleeping bags the Deans had left behind after bolting out on Hallie's second night in town. Gasping for breath now, she grabbed the closest one and ran to the walls to attempt to rub away the flames.

But it was no use. The fire was spreading much faster than Hallie could put it out, eating away at the ample fuel the room provided. The smoke had filled the entire top half of the basement. She needed air, and had to sink to the ground to get it. She made her way closer to Marc. Smoke choked her. There was nothing left that she could do, except maybe say good-bye.

Even as her field of vision narrowed, she saw feet bounding down the stairs. She had to be hallucinating, because the shoes looked like the brown orthopedics that belonged to Ula.

With Hallie's last surge of strength, she flipped over and found herself staring right up into the wrinkly, triumphant face of Ula Blackboro.

"Don't worry, dear," Ula said, gesturing to the men that followed her down the stairs "I've brought the cavalry—Tippy Canoe's finest."

45

Wrapped in a warm blanket, Hallie watched two sets of light disappearing: one set hauling Kenny off for what was sure to be a long and unpleasant stay in a cell somewhere. The second belonging to the ambulance, now whisking Marc off to the hospital. It had an eerie symmetry to her first night in town. She should be dead; there was no way around it. By any logic, she should either be burnt toast or Swiss cheese.

I did what you wanted me to, Finn, she thought. *I came to this town, I helped with the Christmas festival, and I called Marc over like I thought you wanted me too. Everything has gotten progressively worse. And now look at your precious store; it's burnt worse than my Sunday pot roast.*

She hadn't noticed Deputy Greathouse sidling up beside her. "You sure are one lucky lady," he said after whistling one long and low note.

Hallie wished she could arch one eyebrow up, because it was perfect for moments like this. "Are you kidding me? My store is ruined, and your son was shot trying to protect me. Which part of that was lucky?"

"The part where if you hadn't called Marc over—and don't worry, he's grown so I'm not gonna ask—you probably would have been shot. Or worse, trapped in the upstairs apartment when Kenny torched your building."

Hallie tried to interject, but Lyle just put up a hand and kept right on. "Or the part where Ula is a horrible busybody, so she was driving by to see what you were up to. Or that somehow, even with her cataracts, she saw a suspicious figure coming in through the basement with a gas can and called me to investigate. We were able to put out the fire before it reached the door to the main floor. The basement will need a lot of work, but the rest of the building was saved. I call that more than lucky. You must have angels watching out for you." And with that, he gave Hallie a fatherly pat on the back, hurried to his car, and sped off—most likely to meet his son at he hospital

Humbled, Hallie stared upward with tears freezing on her lashes, sending a silent prayer of thanks to her personal angel. Then she sent another prayer to his boss, pleading for Marc's recovery.

Two days later, Hallie was hauling burnt debris from the basement. Lyle had been right; the damage was confined to downstairs and wasn't not as bad as she initially thought. There was a lot of smoke damage, but the structural integrity was still good. Unfortunately, the wood detailing was mostly a casualty to the fire—except for the craftsman door with the blue glass handle. Selfishly, she was grateful it had survived, since it had come to mean a great deal to her. She planned on using it as the new door for the upstairs studio. She gave the knob an affectionate brush on her way up the stairs with her latest armload for the dumpster.

Hallie's phone was squeezed between her shoulder and right ear, and her new best friend was on the other end of the line. "Are you sure you don't need any help? I could have Megan drive me over and—"

"And supervise because your broken leg prevents you from

going up and down the stairs?" Hallie finished, laughing. "Thank you for the thought. But really, I can handle things here."

She brushed the hair out of her face, leaving a long, sooty mark on her forehead. "What I could use help with is dealing with the asinine hospital bureaucracy. No one will give me an update on Marc. I'm not family, so they won't let me see him or even let know if he's awake yet."

"Head wounds can be serious business. Ula told me that he's still in the medically-induced coma the doctors put him in so the brain swelling could go down," Andrea said somberly.

"And just how the heck does Ula know that?"

A small chuckle traveled across the phone lines. "Haven't you learned by now? Ula knows *everything.*"

Thank goodness for that, Hallie supposed. But still, this was maddening. She wanted—no, needed—to do something. Marc had saved her life. The least she could do was visit him in the hospital. Even more than that was an elephant-sized weight of guilt gnawing at her stomach. The Greathouse Christmas tree farm was still going to be auctioned off in four days. And the man who needed to do something about that was stuck in a coma because of her. Now that news had spread about the property's real worth, there were prospectors chomping at the bit for the tax lien to be fulfilled. Marc was going to wake up and find out the family farm was gone. If he woke up, that is.

"There has to be some way . . . " Hallie's voice trailed off as she locked her gaze onto the ugly wreath Marc had brought over for her. No, that couldn't work, right? Maybe . . . with a little better execution.

"Hey, Andrea. Can you call everybody you know for an emergency meeting at the Greathouse tree farm?" A mischievous grin spread across her sooty face.

"Why?" Andrea inquired.

"I'll explain it when we get there. Oh, and can you give me Ula's number? I have a crowd I need her to rile up for me."

46

"Simmer down, everybody. I said simmer down. That means you too, Billy Black. Just because you've gotten taller while I've gotten smaller does not mean that I won't take you across my knee."

The crowd responded with raucous laughter at Ula's opening remarks, especially given that Billy Black was in his sixties. There were probably a hundred townsfolk that answered the call for the last-minute meeting at the Greathouse farm. Pretty impressive, considering it was nearly freezing out and the skies threatened to shake a fresh coat of dandruff from the clouds.

"Now, some of you are probably wondering why you've been summoned out here. The rest of you are probably wondering where the refreshments are." She paused to allow the crowd to chuckle a bit more.

"I'm here to tell you that the rumors are true. It was my heroic efforts that kept Main Street from burning to the ground." There was an audible snort from Deputy Greathouse and the other members of the volunteer firefighter team. Ula ignored them and kept right on going. "But our town isn't safe yet. It's still in danger from the sin as old as time itself."

Hallie watched the audience as they shifted uncomfortably. It was clear that she had made the right choice about calling Ula in. She had the crowd on the edge of their snowshoes.

Ula lowered her voice both in pitch and volume, leaning right into the microphone. "I'm talking about *greed*. Kenny Petrola, otherwise known as Flash, might have been nuttier than squirrel scat, but it was greed that pushed him over the edge. He was desperate to buy this land because, as fate would have it, it's the only piece of land for a hundred miles that's suitable for reclamation by the Blue Moon mine."

That sure got a reaction. There were shocked gasps, and a low murmur settled among the people. "His plan was to ruin these trees so that our mayor couldn't pay off the tax lien, and so that no one else would want the land either. If we don't band together as a town, then by week's end, this land will go to auction. And the deputy and the mayor will lose their family farm."

From the back of the crowd came a shout, "Why should we care what happens to that crooked politician?"

There were a few noises of assent. But thankfully, there were more shushing noises than "yeahs." Hallie's heart leapt into her throat. This was only going to work if she could get the crowd to be sympathetic to Marc's cause.

Standing on her tippy toes, Ula peeked over the crowd and spied a cranky old woman in the back that had spoken. "Was that you, Norma Jean? Mayor Greathouse has worked his behind off for this town, and you want to abandon him after a moment of poor judgment? Shame on you. You should be grateful that we've all managed to overlook *your* faults—because they are numerous."

The woman looked to the ground, properly cowed. *Whew,* thought Hallie. *Remind me not to tick off Ula Blackboro.*

"Haven't you been paying attention? The mining company needs this land awfully bad. If Kenny—who had a few branches missing off his family tree—figured it out, then don't you think Blue Moon's figured it by now too? They're going to come in and scoop up this land for pennies at the tax auction on Saturday. What do you think will happen then? They're going to descend on us like locusts, piping and hauling all that toxic sludge from the mine down through our town to bury it into our city's soil. With their shoddy safety record, what do you think the odds are that they can safely dispose of all that crud?" Ula shouted into the audience.

The fervor started to build. People began shouting out the wrongs Blue Mining company had committed. It was exponential. One complaint became two. Two became four. And so on.

"My husband was caught in that cave-in five years ago."

"My son's been sick, and they never paid no disability."

"They left us high and dry, and now they want us to keep their mess for 'em."

"I say we tell 'em heck no. Keep their glow-in–the-dark goo away from Tippy Canoe."

The last complaint began a chant, low and steady. But it grew and escalated. "Keep the goo out of Tippy Canoe. Keep the goo out of Tippy Canoe."

Bowing as much as her elderly body allowed, Ula Blackboro ceded the microphone to Hallie, her job done.

Hallie steadied herself. *Here goes nothing.*

"If we want to keep that junk away from here, we need to raise ten thousand dollars and pay off the lien. With the property securely in the hands of Deputy Greathouse, Bob and Betty will be able to keep their greenhouses, and the mining company will have to haul their sludge somewhere else." It was not lost on Hallie that she used the word *we*. Somewhere along the line, this had become her town. And these were her neighbors.

There was a smattering of applause, but someone raised a cry from the middle of the group. "And just how are we supposed to raise ten grand? I can barely pay my mortgage."

There were a few "yeahs" and "me toos." It was a fickle crowd, but Hallie hoped she could sway them.

"For starters, you can buy a tree that you were already planning on buying anyway. It might be a little . . . less full than normal. But you can face that side to the wall. If you don't have any money, that's understandable, but we still need your help. We need your time and talents"— Hallie motioned over to Andrea and Megan to hoist up the Christmas wreath—"to make these to sell to the tourists at the Cave Festival."

As she expected, the crowd chuckled and laughed at the mayor's gaudy gift. The same voice hollered from the center. "Ain't nobody gonna pay a cent for one of those. Why, that there is a crime against Christmas." Apparently everybody else agreed, because the peanut gallery was scoffing Hallie's plan. Just when she was about to retreat and give the mic over to someone else, Matt Teasdale jumped up and took it from her.

"Now wait a minute here. Let's not be so hasty to dismiss this. Tourists pay big bucks for the handmade items. Now, Ms. Stone here might not be very crafty"—there were a few barks of laughter in agreement—"but I know a lot of us are. If I can make those little flies, tying these wreaths should be easy. Judy, Brooklyn, Melora. Come up here for a second."

Hallie felt the strong urge to deny that she had anything to do with the making of the pine beast, but she also didn't want to explain that it was a gift from Marc. The crowd was restless while her tenants and friends worked on the wreath. A few people turned to leave. Maybe this hadn't been such a bright idea after all.

"Ta-da," Judy shouted, hoisting the new wreath high up next to her beehive hair.

Hallie was almost afraid to look. There was stillness in the valley, with only the occasionally *thump* of snow falling off tree limbs. But then a wave of oohs and ahhs spread through the gathering. Somehow, they had turned the big Christmas *don't* into a work of art. The tinsel was tastefully woven and intermixed with the tulle through the pine boughs. The buffalo berries no longer looked like little critter presents, but small little ornaments pierced by the needles. The square shape had even been corrected to make the perfect circle. It looked fantastic. Something you might pick up in a high-end boutique.

Brooklyn and her big belly took center stage. "See folks. If we can fix *that* in under five minutes, with no extra materials, just think of what we can make if we used little fixings from our houses and stores."

There was a pause as the crowd mulled over the possibilities. Though it only lasted under a minute, Hallie felt the ages pass. A positive reaction meant there might just be a way to save the farm. A negative reaction, and well . . .

"I have leftover ribbon and findings from my quilts."

"We are having the stick of cinnamon to give," Mrs. Tumpi piped in.

"Well, shoot. I've got enough berries to fill a bog," Judy offered.

There were still a few holdouts, but the majority of the people present were offering their wares and pointing out useful skills they could provide. A couple of old ladies in the front were arguing over who could make the best bow in the county. Hallie had an idea how to motivate the last few stragglers.

"I'll stop by Plum's and Hers: Chocolates to pick up some refreshments. Deputy Greathouse, if you could organize a group to collect the pine boughs and haul them over to Christiansen's, we can gather there to assemble the wreaths. Hopefully, you won't mind the smoky smell. I've aired it out, but there's still remnants from the fire."

Yep, that did it. Nobody wanted to miss out on the chance to see the scene of the crime. Ula was already leading a group to their cars, talking about how she would give them all the dirt about her heroics on the grand tour.

The crowd dispersed, mobilized with purpose. Hallie breathed a sigh of relief when Andrea came up from behind and tapped her on the shoulder.

"I can't believe that worked," Andrea whispered.

Hallie turned around to greet her friend. "I know, I—"

She froze from her vocals cords to her toenails. Hallie's eyes grew wide and darted around in a panic. About fifty feet behind Andrea stood a big, brown, shaggy moose.

Back away slowly, she said to herself. But her feet would not cooperate.

Andrea was looking at her like she had just sprouted purple polka dots. "Are you having a seizure or something?"

"M . . . muh . . . mooossssse," Hallie hissed.

Andrea started to hobble around to get a glimpse, but Hallie grabbed her elbow. "Don't look. Don't make eye contact. That's when they get you."

Andrea snorted. "It's just a dumb moose. It can't hypnotize you. Why are you so afraid?"

Hallie whispered, so as not to be overheard by the moose. "When I was seven, I was brutally attacked by one."

Now it was Andrea's turn to look shocked. "Oh my gosh, I'm so sorry. Where did a city girl like you run into a live moose?"

"Well, you see, it wasn't technically alive. Or a whole moose. It was just the head. I was running around my uncle's cabin in Yosemite when I hit the wall and knocked his big moose head trophy off the wall. Its antlers got stuck in the hardwood and pinned me to the ground. I was trapped, staring into its big, blank, black eyes for hours until my uncle came home. I've had nightmares ever since."

Hallie had only ever shared that story with Finn, but his stoic reaction was nothing like Andrea's. Her eyes bulged a bit, probably sharing Hallie's horror. Next, her lips clamped together, perhaps to suppress a scream. Then, a puff of air and spit escaped directly into Hallie's face.

Andrea's giggles disintegrated into guffaws that shook loose the birds from the trees. Incidentally, they scared the moose off too. She was laughing so hard that she lost her balance and tipped over into the snow bank.

"I'm sor . . . sorry," Andrea gasped out, trying to catch a full breath. "Help me up. I'm stuck." She had landed bum first into the embankment, and she seemed wedged in tight.

Hallie turned to pretend to walk away. "You're on your own, pal. Serves you right for laughing at me. I'll have you know I've spent years and thousands of dollars in therapy over that. It was an extremely traumatic event."

"Over a mangy moose head and plastic button eyes." Andrea started laughing all over again.

That was it—Hallie was out of there. At least the moose was gone, so there was a clear path to her car. As she clicked the unlock button, she could still hear Andrea's giggle fit intermixed with oomphs from Megan trying to haul her out of the snow. The glass of the driver's side window showed Hallie her reflection. There might have been a small smile there. Maybe it had been a little funny after all.

Somebody, not a moose, suddenly appeared in the reflection behind her. She squeaked and turned around. Lyle Greathouse was standing in front of her, deputy hat in hand.

"I really can't thank you enough for everything you're doing, Ms. Stone. I hate to mention this, but even if we raise ten thousand dollars, it won't be enough. The tax debt is thirty-five thousand," Lyle said, his voice tinged with shame.

Hallie put her hand on his broad shoulder. "I know. I wanted to talk to you about that. I'd invited Marc over that night to talk about hiring him to do renovations to the basement. Now, after the fire, they will be more extensive than I had planned. But the insurance will cover it." She reached into her purse and pulled out the $25,000 cashier's check she'd had the bank draft for her that morning. "If you think it would be all right, I'll give the check out to you in advance. Then when Marc recovers, you and he can come over and get started."

Lyle was clearly at a loss for words. His lips moved, but nothing came out. A few tears leaked from the corners of his eyes.

Hallie placed the check into his hand and helped him close his fingers around it. In the moment, she felt inspired to give him a hug. All the fresh-small town air must be getting to her, she decided.

"What if he doesn't wake up?" Lyle protested quietly into the embrace.

"Hush. He'll come around when he's ready."

It was Christmas Eve, and all the residents of Tippy Canoe were gathered inside Barefoot Cave for the annual Christmas Banquet—and to celebrate the end of the extremely successful Cave Festival. This was Tippy Canoe's most anticipated social occasion of the year. Not that there was much competition. But the cave, the carolers, the live Nativity, and the hot snow-chocolate made this year's even more special than the others. Everyone was in a jolly mood. The influx of cash from the festival meant that businesses could survive for a while longer—until maybe Ula came up with another brilliant media debacle the town could take advantage of. And if the town needed another reason to celebrate, Andrea had told Hallie that the fortieth student had requested a transfer the day before. The academy would survive.

Betty Greathouse had asked Hallie to sit with her. This was the one time of year that Bob, her attorney-husband, always abandoned her. Bob was sitting on a red, plush bench at the end of the cavern ballroom, dressed in a Santa suit.

Hallie saw the town's children were lined up to meet Santa and to tell him their Christmas wishes. Parents snapped photos, and as usual, the smaller children cried while the older children shyly announced the list of toys they hoped to find under the tree. When they were finished, Santa's elves reached into a large, red sack and handed each child a paper bag. The bags held oranges, shell peanuts, and candy.

Oddly, next to Santa there was a table lined with decorated cakes that no one was touching. Hallie was about to ask what they were for when Betty spoke first.

"Bob and I were pretty impressed that you managed to raise enough money to pay off the taxes before the auction. We really can't thank you enough. We had all but given up."

"Well, this is supposed to be a secret, so don't tell Ula. But Mrs. Tidewater actually purchased more than half of the wreaths for the governor's mansion. I think that if the governor found out where they came from, and whom he indirectly helped to support, he might have a coronary," Hallie confided in a low tone.

"Oh-ho! That's too rich. You're right. If Ula ever found out, she'd hold another press conference." Betty's laughter dwindled away, and she suggested they go over and check out the food.

Next to the live Nativity—where Brooklyn made the cutest Mary—a line of tables practically groaned under the weight of the feast spread upon it. Hallie had never seen anything like it. There were hundreds of homemade rolls and at least two dozen jars of homemade preserves and home-churned butter to go with them. There was an entire table devoted to yams: some with toasted pecans; a few with pine nuts; but most with marshmallows, brown sugar, and butter.

There were serving bowls brimming with delicious savory soups. Dishes of carmelized brussel sprouts with pine nuts, leafy greens, fruit compotes, and cranberry-orange relishes. Yet another table featured dozens of pies of every kind.

"Not to be missed," Betty said, pointing Hallie to a particular vegetable dish. "Bob's glazed winter carrots. At the end of summer, he piles straw over them and leaves them under the snow. For weeks, they sit quietly in the ground with nothing to do but develop their sugars. If you've never had a winter carrot before, prepare yourself for a treat—like candy, I tell you."

Sure enough, Betty had not spoken wrong. The carrots were amazing, their flavor better than any carrot Hallie had ever tasted before.

On the last table was a selection of what appeared to be some kind of raspberry trifle, also new to Hallie. "Raspberry Christmas Crunch, a local favorite," Betty informed her. The dish consisted of a crushed, baked, butter-pretzel crust topped with layers of raspberries in gelatin, whipped farm cream, fresh-cut pineapple, and cream cheese. Hallie made sure to extensively sample each and every one. Just to be polite, of course.

"I've learned one thing here this afternoon," Hallie said to Betty with a laugh. "This town can cook. And when Tippy Canoe-ers eat, they mean it. I've never seen anything like this."

"Shhh," Betty said dismissively. "We teach the younger generations to work hard and play hard. Christmas is about family, and Tippy Canoe is a family. It's always been this way."

Hallie thought fondly about how she was becoming a part of that family.

Betty added, "Looks like Bob's almost through the line of kids up there. That means the cakewalk will start soon. My favorite part. Look forward to it all year. I'd better get up there. By tradition, Santa's last guest is always his wife. I'll bring you back a bag of candy."

Hallie was baffled by the image of walking cakes, but before she could ask any questions, Betty was guiding her through the crowd to stand in line for Santa.

"Who is this eye-catching lass?" Bob said through the snow-white beard hiding his face. Hallie noted that the noise in the cave had hushed, and all eyes were on the couple. A chair had been arranged so that Betty could sit next to Bob.

"And what are you wanting from Santa this year, missy?" Bob said deeply with cheer in his voice.

"You'd think by now you wouldn't have to ask," Betty replied, a gleam in her eye.

Hallie caught on that she was witnessing a time-honored tradition.

"It will be that again?" Bob said with mock surprise. "You're sure? There's still time to change your mind, after all these years." The crowd laughed.

"I've come this far. It's too much work to start over again," Betty said, again to the delight of the crowd. "I guess I'll keep sticking with what I've got."

And then Betty and Bob kissed for all to see. Cameras flashed and applause erupted across the hall.

"Santa kissed her," Hallie heard one little girl say to her mother.

Hallie grinned and turned back to get seconds on her plate. *You know what they say,* she thought. *"In for a pound, in for five pounds."* She reached for a roll and came back with a hand. She and Barb had been aiming for the same one.

Hallie tried to drop Barb's hand faster than a hot coal, but Barb wouldn't let go. They hadn't seen each other since the incident at Plum's with the letter. Barb's face didn't appear any less grumpy.

She still had a scowl that creased her forehead when she said something that came out like, "Imph furryedfor huddi prews."

With the announcer on the PA talking about lining up for cakes, plus the squeal of children, Hallie couldn't hear what was said.

"What was that? I couldn't understand you," Hallie said, still trying to extricate her hand.

"I'm sorry I misjudged you!" Barb shouted into the room that of course, just seconds ago had become dead silent.

Barb's face turned the exact shade of the Raspberry Crunch, and the room broke out into spontaneous applause and chuckles. Barb finally let go of Hallie's hand and stalked away in embarrassment.

Andrea made eye contact with Hallie across the room. Andrea looked like she was about go after Barb, but Hallie held up her hand, indicating that she had it handled. It was time for this to be settled. She caught up with Barb on her way out of the cave.

"Barb, wait up," Hallie said breathlessly. "I just wanted to say I'm sorry too. I know it's clichéd, but let's start over." Hallie held out her hand. "Hi, my name is Hallie Stone. I'm the new owner of Christiansen's." At the last second, she decided to go all in and share her plans with Barb. "I'm renovating the basement to host a small art gallery showcasing some of the local talent. I'm also building a little studio apartment down there. I don't suppose you'd know of any brothers that could use a place to stay in the winter?"

For a second, Hallie worried she had misstepped again, because Barb had still not accepted her outstretched hand. Before she had a chance to worry much, Barb yanked her arm nearly from the socket and pulled Hallie into a rib-crushing hug. The woman was much stronger than her age or looks suggested.

"Do you mean it? I can't afford to pay much, but it would sure ease my mind to know the boys had a safe place to be when it storms."

The lack of oxygen was starting to make everything go dim. Barb must have realized something was wrong when Hallie didn't respond.

"I'm sorry. I didn't mean to smother you."

Hallie coughed. "That's all right. Don't worry about the rent, either. I've had Bob Greathouse draw up a lease agreement for a dollar a month. That way, the twins can pay it themselves and feel more independent. It won't be ready this winter, since we might have to wait a while until Marc gets back on his feet and does the remodeling."

Barb's face erupted into a grin that looked absolutely foreign on her face. "Oh, you never know." She extended an arm around Hallie's shoulders and started turning her around. "Did you know we have a time-honored tradition at this party? Every year, the sitting mayor comes dressed as St. Joer to lead the cake walk."

At Hallie's puzzled look, Barb nodded over to the crowd gathering at the entrance. Standing on tippy-toes, Hallie finally caught a glimpse once the herd thinned out a little.

Outside the cave, hopping out of the hay wagon and making his way toward her, was Marc Greathouse—wearing one boot and dressed in the old-time getup of Peter St. Joer, founder of the town and discoverer-extraordinaire of Barefoot Cavern.

The world was completely silent.

Hallie couldn't bring herself to meet his gaze.

The chilled air felt thicker than the Christmas gelatin. Everyone could sense the importance in this one moment.

Except for the Seuss twins, that is. They erupted into a giggle fit and took turns running around the cakes. "Cake-walk, mock-rock, the icing's on the clock, tick-tock," sang out one of the twins. "Icing-splicing, puddin' and pie, I love cake and that ain't no lie," replied the other twin.

"Oh, for heaven's sake," Barb said, exasperated. Then she ran over to shush them.

The Deans weren't the only ones giggling; the whole town erupted into laughter. Marc and Hallie too. It was actually the perfect icebreaker.

"I don't suppose I could interest you in a crash course on cake walks?" Marc asked, extending his arm once he reached her.

She ignored his attempt at levity. "You're out of the hospital," she said lamely.

"Yes," he said, just as lamely. He did not take his gaze away from hers.

"You almost died."

"Yup."

Hallie reached up and lifted his leather brim hat just enough to see the wound the bullet had made. She traced the line from his temple to his forehead. With a grin, she tapped him right between the eyes. "So does everything still work up in here?"

It was his turn to ignore her attempt at humor. "Dad filled me in. Told me you and my wreath managed to save the farm after all."

"Well, you can thank the town for the wreaths. And as for the advance . . . as soon as you're up to it, you'll be spending a lot of time in my shop." Hallie's face turned bright red when she realized how that came out.

"Yes, ma'am." Marc chuckled and tipped his hat with a wink. Arm in arm, he led Hallie over to the cake-walk stage.

Around the tables, Christmas-themed words written on construction paper had been taped to the cavern floor to form an enormous circle. Marc spoke into the microphone so everyone could hear, and directed participants to choose one piece of paper to stand on. The school choir—relieved that the academy had been saved—had been singing "Joy to the World" all night. They began the song again, and the circle started to move. The audience clapped in time. After twenty or so seconds, the music halted without warning. Marc pulled a slip of paper from a glass gallon jar.

"Joy," Marc read loudly. And then the person standing on the piece of construction paper printed with the word *joy* jumped up and down. Apparently, that made her the winner of the first round, allowing her to get first choice of the cakes. Everyone watched to see which cake would be the first to be picked—a sort of honor for whoever had decorated the cake, Hallie realized.

Having selected a cake, the winner joined Marc and held up her choice for the crowd to see. Marc held the mic for her her and asked her to read out the name of the cake-maker and title or theme of the decorations. Everyone "oohed" and "ahhed" appreciatively, followed by enthusiastic applause.

As this was going on, Hallie looked around the circle of

cake-walkers and realized she knew many of the people. Both Melora and David Post were here. Brooklyn Teasdale, still dressed as Mary, was in the circle. So was Damon Oster. Barb was walking the circle with Lyman and Lehman—all three sharing one paper game marker on the floor. Also in the mix was Andrea, standing next to the reporter from Bozeman. *Apparently, Andrea has chosen to seize the day after all*, Hallie thought with a smile.

"Heavenly choir, hark those herald angels sing," Marc said in a polished, energetic, speaking-to-the-town voice. The music began again, and then stopped half a minute later. Before Marc had a chance to shout out the word on the paper, someone from the circle yelled "Baby!"

"No. Close! The word is actually 'nativity,'" Marc answered good-naturedly.

Hallie could see the speaker now. It was Brooklyn Teasdale, holding her belly and standing in a puddle. "No, I mean the baby is coming. Now!"

The room exploded into action, her husband Mathew rushing over from his place with the choir to gather up his wife. "What should we do? What should we do?"

The ever-helpful Ula had the answer. "Well, get her to the hospital, you numbskull."

In the excitement, the cake walk was all but forgotten. Small children—and Lyman and Lehman—started leaving fingerprints in the icing while the adults were occupied. Hallie perched herself on a nearby empty table with a broad smile.

"What's that look about?" Marc asked, handing her a hot snow-choclate and settling in beside her.

"I just realized that I won't be the newest girl in town any-more," she said coyly, taking a drink without even worrying whether it contained dirty snow.

"That's true," he replied. Then he grasped her empty hand. "But you might just be my favorite."

Hallie took a moment to look down at their interlaced fingers. They weren't wrinkled or spotted with age. But who knew what they might look like in time?

She hopped off the table, still holding Marc's hand. She pulled him off with her. "So . . . how do you feel about Malibu beach?"

Recipes

Warm Winter Apples with Gjetost Cheese

This recipe uses winter apples from the cellar or garage. Store apples can also be used.

winter apples
Gjetost cheese
parchment paper

Core the apples. Slice the apples horizontally into slices about a quarter-inch thick. Slices will be a circle with a hole in the middle. Top with a slice of gjetost cheese, which is a Norwegian goat's-milk cheese that is dark brown in color and tastes like caramel. Put apple slices topped with cheese onto a parchment-lined baking sheet. Place in oven and broil for 90 seconds until cheese has begun to melt and apples have begun to brown. Serve warm. This makes an unbelievable caramel apple hor d'oeuvres.

Winter Lettuce Salad

This recipe is entirely from the winter garden.

Mix of winter lettuces, baby chard leaves, beet greens, baby spinach leaves (whatever greens you have in your winter garden)
1 carrot

Wash and spin-dry your blend of winter greens. Peel and wash carrot. Then use peeler to peel the entire carrot into paper-thin slices. Mix with salad greens. Serve with preferred salad dressing.

Scottish Eggs

This recipe uses eggs from your backyard chickens. Bread crumbs can be made from homemade, natural-yeast bread. Can be doubled.

6 eggs
1 pound package of uncooked breakfast sausage
1 cup seasoned bread crumbs
aluminum foil

Boil eggs; cool and peel. Wrap completely with raw breakfast sausage. Roll in seasoned bread crumbs. Bake at 375 degrees on a foil-lined baking sheet until sausage is crisp and brown, about 25–30 minutes. Serve hot.

Roasted Carrots

This recipe uses carrots from the winter garden.

8 medium carrots
3 Tbsp., plus ¼ cup Italian dressing
tin foil
⅓ cup Parmesan cheese

Peel carrots and cut each carrot into thirds. Toss carrots with 3 tablespoons Italian dressing. Line casserole dish with tin foil. Cover with foil and bake 20 minutes at 450 degrees. Remove cover and bake another 20 minutes or until carrots are tender-crisp, stirring every few minutes. Remove from oven and toss with ¼ cup Italian dressing and Parmesan cheese. Serve warm.

Borscht

This recipe uses beets, carrots, onion, potatoes, and cabbage from the winter garden. Tomatoes in winter can be canned or from the cellar or garage.

13 cups water
4 carrots
1 large onion
2 tsp. salt
3 potatoes
3 bay leaves
5 tsp. beef bouillon
1 clove garlic
6 red beets
1 small cabbage
1 Tbsp. vinegar
1 pinch brown sugar
pepper to taste
1 4-oz. can tomato sauce, or three fresh tomatoes

Boil water and add diced carrots, chopped onions, salt, diced potatoes, bay leaves, bouillon, and garlic. Meanwhile, dice and sauté beets. Add beets to vegetables. When beets have colored the vegetables in the boiling pot, add shredded cabbage, vinegar, brown sugar, pepper, and tomatoes or tomato sauce. Simmer until vegetables are tender. Serve with sour cream.

Warm Mushroom Potato Salad

This recipe uses potatoes and onion from the winter garden.

8 slices bacon
5 baby yellow or red potatoes
1 small yellow onion
butter
6 oz. button mushrooms
½ pound fresh or frozen green beans
1 small yellow summer squash
1 small zucchini
sea salt
3 Tbsp. water

Cook and drain bacon. Cut potatoes and onion into very thin slices. Sauté in butter until just tender. Add whole mushrooms and green beans. Stir and cook for two more minutes. Add squash, zucchini, and sea salt with three tablespoons of water. Cover pan for 1–2 minutes, or until squash is tender. Remove from heat. Add crumbled bacon and serve immediately.

Warm Pine Nut & Brussels Sprouts Salad

This recipe uses brussels sprouts from the winter garden.

3 cups radicchio, cut into a large dice
2 cups brussels sprouts, cut into quarters
½ cup raw pine nuts
dash of salt
pepper to taste
butter

Sauté all ingredients in a skillet with butter until just warmed. Serve.

Chowder

This recipe uses onion and potatoes from the winter garden.

1 cup diced celery	1 Tbsp. flour
1 diced onion	1½ tsp. salt
4 medium diced potatoes	1 quart half-and-half cream
water	pepper to taste
1 stick butter	diced ham or cooked bacon

Add vegetables into pot and barely cover with water. Bring to a boil and simmer until tender. Meanwhile, in a saucepan, melt better. Stir in flour and cook for 1–2 minutes. Stir in salt and half-and-half and bring to a boil for a minute or until sauce begins to thicken. When vegetables are tender, pour sauce into undrained vegetables. Add pepper and meat. Serve.

Tomato Lime Chickpea Soup

This recipe uses onion, carrot, and winter squash from the winter garden.

water
1 cup brown rice
½ cup dried chickpeas (garbanzo beans)
¼ cup dried lentils
¼ cup barley
⅛ cup whole wheat
1 tsp. salt
pepper to taste
1 large onion
6 carrots
1 small pumpkin or winter squash
1 quart fresh or frozen tomatoes
2 Tbsp. basil
1 Tbsp. bouillon powder
1 lime
4 bay leaves

Fill a 4-quart pot one-third full with water and boil. Add brown rice, chickpeas, lentils, barley, wheat, salt, and pepper. While these boil, cut up and add onion, carrots, and squash. Into blender add fresh or frozen tomatoes and two cups of soup water. Puree. Blend in basil and bouillon powder. Pour into soup pot. To the pot, add the juice of the lime and bay leaves. Total cooking time is about 90 minutes or until lentils, chickpeas, and rice are tender.

Kale Chips

This recipe uses fresh kale from the winter garden.

1 bunch of kale leaves   olive oil
sea salt or table salt   parchment paper or tin foil

Remove the ribs from the kale leaves and discard. In a bowl, lightly drizzle a couple of tablespoons of olive oil over the kale leaves. Sprinkle with sea salt and toss. Bake on a cookie sheet covered with parchment or tin foil at 275 degrees for about 20 minutes.

Winter Garden Omelet Bar

*This recipe is entirely from the winter garden,
except for cheese and meat choices.*

grated cheese: Parmesan, Swiss, or your favorite
garden fresh root vegetable, grated: potato, carrot, beet, turnip, squash, or any root vegetable
chopped greens: collards, kale, chard, beet tops, green onions, Chinese cabbage, spinach, mache (corn salad)
chopped: onions, broccoli raab, asparagus, tomatoes, cabbage, brussels sprouts
peas, oregano, chives, pepper, salt
pre-cooked proteins: Italian sweet sausage, breakfast sausage, Polish sausage, crisp bacon, chopped ham, shredded chicken or turkey, pepperoni, or Canadian bacon
eggs

Let each person put together their own omelet choices. Use one egg or two per omelet. Cook each omelet individually in a skillet.

Pioneer Pan Toast

*This recipe uses homemade, natural-yeast bread
and homemade jellies and jams.*

Butter bread and place it buttered-side down in a skillet. Toast on just one side until sizzling and golden brown. May be served with a fried egg or breakfast sausage or topped with homemade jam or jelly.

Succulent
Slow-Roasted Vegetables

This recipe is entirely from the winter garden

chopped root vegetables, as available: potatoes, carrots, onions, cabbage chunks, brussels sprouts (whole), turnips, beets, rutabaga, winter squash, pumpkin, parsnips
olive oil
dried herbs, as available: rosemary, thyme, sage, marjoram, caraway, parsley, basil
garlic, pepper, sea salt (optional)
butter

In a glass baking dish, combine root vegetables, rough-chopped, to approximately uniform chunks. Drizzle with olive oil and stir to coat. Top to taste with fresh or dried herbs, according to your preference. Chopped garlic, white and black pepper, and sea salt also add flavor. Bake at 375 degrees for 60 minutes or until vegetables are easily speared with a fork. Drizzle with melted butter and serve hot.

Butter Soup

This recipe from my great-grandmother Lexis Dastrup Warnock is entirely from the winter garden

3–4 potatoes
3–4 carrots
1 large onion
water
1–2 Tbsp. butter
salt and pepper

Cut vegetables into chunks. Barely cover with water in a pot and boil until tender. Salt and pepper to taste and add a couple of tablespoons of butter before serving.

English Popovers

This recipe uses backyard eggs, where available.

2 tsp. butter
2 eggs
1 cup flour
½ tsp. salt
1¼ cup milk

Melt butter and whisk with eggs, milk, and salt. Mix in flour until barely blended. Pour into greased muffin tin, filling each cup three-quarters full. Bake at 450 degrees for 15 minutes, then reduce temperature to 350 degrees and bake for another 20 minutes. Serve hot with butter and jam or jelly.

Spinach Artichoke Dip

This recipe uses fresh spinach from the winter garden.

1 8-oz. pkg. cream cheese
1 large handful spinach
¾ cup sour cream
garlic salt
pepper
½ cup Parmesan cheese
1 small can artichoke hearts

Soften cream cheese and mix with spinach, sour cream, garlic salt, pepper, and Parmesan cheese. Chop artichoke hearts and add to taste. Heat in oven at 300 degrees for ten minutes or until warm. Serve with party crackers.

Cabbage and Potatoes with Bacon

This recipe uses cabbage, onion, potatoes, and carrots from the winter garden.

½ half head of cabbage
8 strips of bacon
3 potatoes
1 carrot
2 medium onions
¼ cup water
1 Tbsp. vinegar
salt
pepper

Shred cabbage. Cook bacon. Remove bacon from pan to drain, leaving bacon fat in pan. Into bacon fat, add diced potatoes and carrot and cook until browned. Add chopped onions and cook until tender. Add cabbage, water, vinegar, salt, pepper. Cover pan and cook until cabbage is wilted. Cut up cooked bacon and add back into pan just before removing pan from heat. Serve.

Pumpkin Pie

This recipe uses a pumpkin from the winter cellar or garage, and backyard eggs when available.

1 medium sugar pumpkin
water
3 eggs
1 cup brown sugar
1½ cup cream
2 tsp. pumpkin pie spice
2 unbaked pie crusts

Using a knife, cut a small hole into the top of the pumpkin, about the size of a dime (simply twisting a steak knife will easily make the hole). This hole will vent steam from the pumpkin while the pumpkin bakes. Fill a casserole dish with ¼ inch of water and set the pumpkin in the dish. Place the dish in the oven and bake at 350 degrees until the pumpkin is soft. This will take about an hour. After the pumpkin cools, scrape the flesh from the pumpkin shell. Put the pumpkin flesh in a blender and add eggs, brown sugar, cream, and pumpkin pie spice. Blend until smooth. Fill two pie crusts. Bake at 425 degrees for 15 minutes, then reduce temperature to 350 degrees and continue to bake another 45 minutes. Pies may also be frozen before baking and baked at a later time.

Winter Squash Curry

This recipe uses squash, potatoes, carrots, onion, and apples from the winter garden and cellar or garage.

1 winter squash (any kind)
1 large potato
1 medium onion
2 carrots
2 Tbsp. butter
2 Tbsp. flour
2 tsp. curry powder
dash of salt
1½ cups milk
2 apples

Dice vegetables and boil until tender; drain. Meanwhile, melt butter in a pan. Stir in flour and cook for one minute. Add curry power and salt. Stir. Add milk and bring to a bowl for one minute or until sauce begins to thicken. Add cooked vegetables. Cut and dice apples and add to sauce. Serve over rice. For a milder curry, reduce curry powder by one-half teaspoon.

Stevia Hot Chocolate

This recipe uses stevia from the garden or greenhouse. Stevia is an herb that is 300 times sweeter than refined sugar.

1 cup milk
5 leaves stevia (fresh or dried)
½ tsp. unsweetened cocoa powder

Warm up cup of milk. Add stevia leaves and cocoa powder. Stir.

Christmas Raspberry Crunch

This recipe uses absolutely nothing from the winter garden. But it is one of my very favorite holiday indulgences.

1 8-oz. package raspberry gelatin
3 cups boiling water
1 10-oz. package frozen raspberries
1 fresh pineapple, trimmed
2 cups crushed pretzels
3 Tbsp. sugar
½ cup butter
1 8-oz. package softened cream cheese
⅔ cup sugar
1 pint whipping cream
½ pint whipping cream for topping (optional)

Mix gelatin into boiling water and mix in frozen raspberries. Put gelatin-raspberry mixture into fridge until syrupy. Meanwhile, cut pineapple into small chunks. Set aside to drain juice. Crush pretzels with rolling pin. Heat oven to 400 degrees. Mix sugar with melted butter and crushed pretzels to make a crust. Press into bottom of 9 x 13 baking dish. Bake 5 minutes and cool. In a bowl, beat cream cheese and sugar. Whip cream to heavy peaks and fold into cream cheese and sugar. Mix in pineapple. Spread mixture over cooled crust. Pour syrupy gelatin mixture from fridge over cream cheese layer. Refrigerate until set. Add another layer of whipped cream over the top if desired.

* About the Authors *

Caleb Warnock is the author of four books. You can find him at calebwarnock.blogspot.com.

Betsy Schow has always had a voracious appetite for cheesecake and books, often devouring one a day—on both counts. She conquered the food part in her nonfiction book, *Finished being Fat*, but her addiction to stories only got worse. Soon the tales of others weren't enough to sustain her. Since her own life was full of whimsy (mechanical gremlins that muck up her engine and dust bunnies that go on strike), it only made sense for her to start penning fiction. Betsy lives with her husband and their two little monsters in Utah, where she is a contributor for the local paper and a creative thinking coach at an elementary school. Visit betsyschow.com to find out more.